PENGUIN BOOKS

ISOBEL GUNN

Audrey Thomas was born and raised in New York State but has lived and worked on Canada's west coast since 1959. Her short story collections include *Two in the Bush and Other Stories*; *Real Mothers*; *Goodbye Harold, Good Luck*; and *The Wild Blue Yonder*, which won the 1990 Ethel Wilson Fiction Award (the BC Book Prize). She is also the author of a number of highly acclaimed novels, including *Latakia*, *Mrs Blood*, *Songs My Mother Taught Me*, *Intertidal Life* and *Graven Images*. Her most recent novel, *Coming Down from Wa*, was shortlisted for the Governor General's Award and won the Ethel Wilson Prize. Audrey Thomas has also received the Marian Engel Award, the Canada-Australia Prize and the Canada-Scotland Literary Fellowship.

Also by Audrey Thomas

NOVELS

Coming Down from Wa
Graven Images
Intertidal Life
Latakia
Songs My Mother Taught Me
Mrs Blood
Munchmeyer and Prospero on the Island
Blown Figures

SHORT STORIES

The Wild Blue Yonder
Goodbye Harold, Good Luck
Real Mothers
Two in the Bush and Other Stories
Ten Green Bottles
Ladies and Escorts

Isobel Gunn

a novel

Audrey Thomas

PENGUIN BOOKS

PENGUIN BOOKS

Published by the Penguin Group

Penguin Books Canada Ltd, 10 Alcorn Avenue, Toronto, Ontario, Canada M4V 3B2

Penguin Books Ltd, 27 Wrights Lane, London W8 5TZ, England

Penguin Putnam Inc., 375 Hudson Street, New York, New York 10014, U.S.A.

Penguin Books Australia Ltd, Ringwood, Victoria, Australia

Penguin Books (NZ) Ltd, cnr Rosedale and Airborne Roads, Albany,
Auckland 1310, New Zealand

Penguin Books Ltd, Registered Offices: Harmondsworth, Middlesex, England

First published in Viking by Penguin Books Canada Limited, 1999

Published in Penguin Books, 2000

1 3 5 7 9 10 8 6 4 2

*Publishers note: This book is a work of fiction. Names, characters, places and incidents
either are the product of the author's imagination or are used fictitiously, and any resemblance
to actual persons living or dead, events, or locales is entirely coincidental.*

Manufactured in Canada

CANADIAN CATALOGUING IN PUBLICATION DATA

Thomas, Audrey, 1935–
Isobel Gunn: a novel

ISBN 0-14-028516-4

I. Title.

PS8539.H62186 2000   C813'.54   C00-930303-0
PR9199.3.T46186 2000

Visit Penguin Canada's web site at **www.penguin.ca**

To the memory of
George Mackay Brown and
Marie Sutherland Hardy

AUTHOR'S NOTE

I have done a great deal of research for this book, but it is a work of fiction. If there be any historians among my readers, I hope they will forgive any inaccuracies (and the occasional deliberate fiddling with the facts in order to make my story "work").

ACKNOWLEDGEMENTS

I would like to thank the Canada Council for help in beginning this book, the B.C. Arts Council and the Writers' Development Trust for help with subsequent drafts, and the Berton House Committee for my residency in Dawson City, where I became reacquainted with the Northern Lights.

I would also like to thank the following: Judith Hudson Beattie, keeper of the Hudson's Bay Company Archives, Winnipeg; Phil Astley, assistant archivist at the Orkney Archives in Kirkwall (no matter how silly my questions, I always received information and, when back in Canada, a courteous "please do not hesitate to contact me if you have any further queries"); the National Maritime Museum Library at Greenwich; the Imperial War Museum; the British Museum Reading Room; the Edinburgh Central Library; the Scottish Arts Council, which first sent me to Orkney in 1986; Daphne Lorimer of Scorrsdale House, Orphir; Janet

Grainger of Orphir, who went out of her way to take me to and from the bus to Kirkwall every day, making sure I got home in time for my tea; Margaret Griffiths of Galiano Island, for her generosity in lending me virtually all of her Hudson's Bay library, including some books so valuable that they are insured; David Von Epp, for his eighteen-page letter (with drawings) concerning ships and trade guns; Jim Walker, for letting me see his splendid collection of HBC memorabilia and letting me "fire" a trade gun; Ruth Slavin and Jan Thorsen, for minding "the traplines" while I slaved over a final draft in Victoria; Mick and G. English and Ross and Anne Kenway, my neighbours, who know exactly how to keep my spirits up; Aidan McQuillan, for the maps of Hudson Bay and Scotland; Meg Masters, my patient editor; Carole Robertson, my typist (always cheerful); and Wendy and Gordon Ewart of Edinburgh.

And a special thanks to my good friends and research assistants Nick Francis and Carolyn Canfield, for poring over old newspapers at the Colindale Library, books at the Imperial War Museum, maps at Greenwich; for hitchhiking to lectures in Orkney; and for finding the wonderful stone house in St. Margaret's Hope.

GLOSSARY OF TERMS
THAT MAY BE UNFAMILIAR

bere or bere-meal
    a variety of barley, very hardy; ground-up seeds of bere are used for porridge and bannock

bonie-words   a child's goodnight prayers

byre   a cowshed

cabbin   a small house, or (at the Bay) sometimes a large room partitioned off for the men

caisie   a woven basket of heather

capote   a hooded woollen overcoat

cariole   a dogsled, often ornate, designed to carry one person

chanty   chamber-pot

close   a courtyard, an alley or an entrance to a tenement; the passageway giving access to the common stair

cog   a small cask

coolie a woollen cap

creepie a small stool

cruisie a crude oil lamp

cubbie a woven straw basket for holding peats

factor an agent who is appointed to manage property; the chief factor, at the Bay, was in charge of his particular fort, or "factory"

fash trouble; to be fractious or to punish

flanker a projecting extension on the sides of a fortification

fuggis fug, smell

gallery a balcony projecting from the stern of old ships (used as a toilet)

gansey a woollen jersey

gripper a midwife

grootie-buckie a cowrie shell

haar sea-fog

holystone a flat piece of soft sandstone used to scour the wooden decks of a ship

Home Guard the Natives who remained most of the time at the factory, and were attached to it in many ways

hornbook a leaf or page containing a printed alphabet, etc., with a transparent horn covering

hwinckle-faced lantern-jawed

jolly boat a small boat belonging to a ship

kail cabbage (in Scotland); kail runts are the hardened, withered stems of the kail plant

kist	a small chest
lobscouse	a mixture of meat, vegetables and hardtack
lum	a smoke vent; an opening in the roof for light, ventilation and the escape of smoke
mortify	in law: to assign or bequeath lands, property or money in perpetuity; a "mortification school" is created and maintained by such a bequest
neuk-bed	a bed set in the wall
outfit	all the stores and supplies needed for one year
peerie folk	fairies
plantation	a colony, a group
seggies	the yellow flag iris
shallop	an open boat propelled by oars or sails
ship's biscuit	hardtack (a hard, cracker-like biscuit)
shuizly	rubbishy
skrankie	thin, emaciated
spill	a thin strip of wood or twisted paper, used for lighting a fire
tangle	seaweed that grows above the high-water mark
thecking	thatching
trows	trolls
variolation	vaccination with smallpox
weefly	shaky
wynd	a narrow, winding street or lane leading off a main thoroughfare

Sources: *The Concise Scots Dictionary.*
Editor-in-chief, Mairi Robinson.

Funk & Wagnall's Standard College Dictionary,
Cdn. Ed.

The Orkney Word Book. Gregor Lamb.

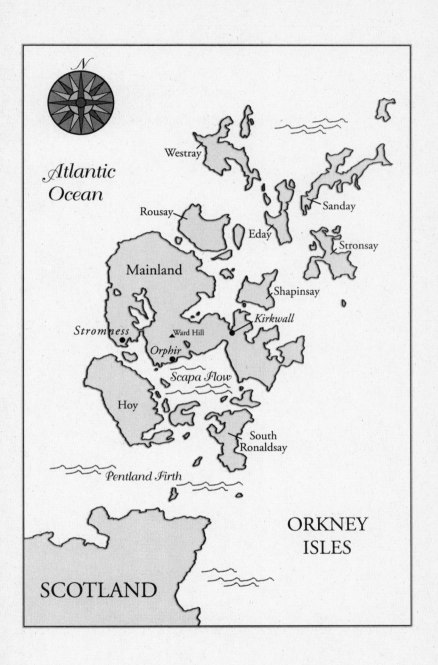

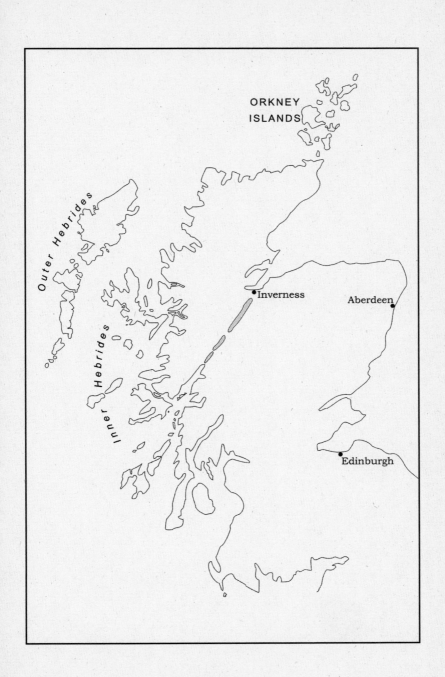

ORKNEY
ISLANDS

Outer Hebrides

Inner Hebrides

•Inverness

Aberdeen•

•Edinburgh

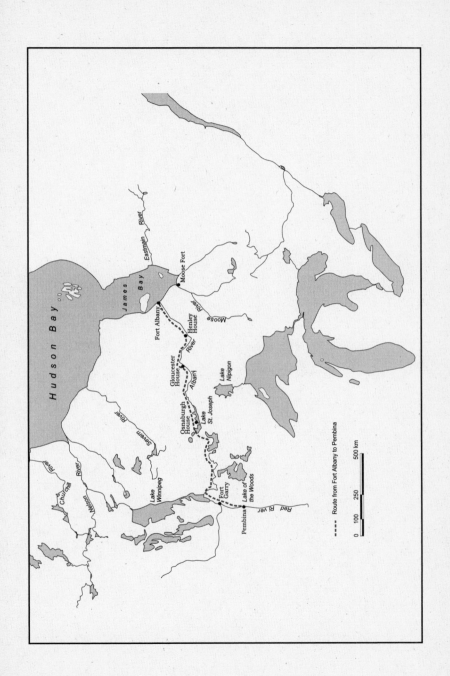

1807, PEMBINAH. DEC. 29TH. An extraordinary affair occurred this morning. One of Mr. Heney's Orkney lads, apparently indisposed, requested me to allow him to remain in my house for a short time. I was surprised at the fellow's demand; however, I told him to sit down and warm himself. I returned to my own room, where I had not been long before he sent one of my people, requesting the favour of speaking with me. Accordingly, I stepped down to him, and was much surprised to find him extended on the hearth, uttering dreadful lamentations; he stretched out his hands toward me, and in piteous tones begged me to be kind to a poor, helpless, abandoned wretch, who was not of the sex I had supposed, but an unfortunate Orkney girl, pregnant, and actually in childbirth. In saying this she opened her jacket, and displayed a beautiful pair of round, white breasts. . . .

——*From the journal of Alexander Henry, the younger, chief factor at the North West Company's post at Pembinah*

Isobel Gunn

a novel

PROLOGUE

THE FIRING OF THE GUNS *had long since announced the arrival of the Company's ships, and by now a considerable crowd of women and children, old men and young boys, as well as the usual fishermen mending nets, stood and gossiped among themselves as the first boatloads of officers and men set out across the harbour for the pier. It was mid-November and the rainy season had begun in these northern isles; the stone houses that lined the long, sinuous principal street of the town glistened with wet and the hills that rose up beyond were a sodden green. But by daybreak the rain had stopped, and now a wan sun appeared occasionally from behind the scudding clouds, picking out the brass buttons on a coat or the scarlet legs of one of the oystercatchers scavenging along the shore. For a moment it lighted on a tallish woman carrying an infant within her shawl. It touched her blaze of red hair and seemed to kindle it, as though her head were on fire. She stood a little apart, rigid with attention, as her eyes searched for and located the figure of the captain of the* Prince of Wales *in the first of the boats. As soon as she was sure, she pushed herself through the knots of people, greeting no one, looking neither left nor right. Wives and sweethearts were already waving and calling out to their men, home at last after three or five or even more years in Rupert's Land, a place known to them only through the yearly letter or the exaggerated tales of old-timers now retired. They did not understand why their men had to go off to such a terrible place, full of savages and other dangers, so far from what they, in their insular way, perceived as civilization. Did not understand, but accepted: the women had no say in the matter.*

Birds rode the winds above the little harbour, and gulls and gannets shrieked, adding to the din. The whole presented a scene to delight the painter's eye and the painter's brush, the finished product to be done up in an ornate gilt frame with a small plaque screwed to the bottom: "The Homecoming at Hamnavoe."

When the tall woman caught up with her quarry, she seized his arm and cried out, "Whit news? Whit news?" He shook her off, but gently, and continued in the direction of the agent's office, where he had much business to attend to—the delivery of the packets of mail, the list of men who had now completed their service and were to be signed off and paid, the requisitioning of fresh water and the few necessities the ship would need on its journey south. They did not stay here long on the inward journey; it was only in June that their arrival signalled a two- or even three-week stopover, as meat and water and other victuals were taken on board according to the Company's requirements for that year. In June there were balls and soirees for the officers and welcoming alehouses for the crews. Now, with a fortune in furs in the hold and his own family awaiting him at home in Kent, Captain Hanwell was anxious to be gone.

But the woman was not to be put off so easily. She matched her stride to his and hurried along beside him.

"Whit news? A letter?"

The captain stopped and shook his head. "No letter. I'm sorry."

"No letter at all?" she cried. "From Magnus? From Mr. Morton?"

"I'm sorry."

She looked at him in disbelief, her mouth an O. "He promised! They both promised."

Captain Hanwell continued to shake his head.

"No word at all?"

"None."

She gripped the child within the shawl so tightly that it began to wail. The captain, startled, looked down at the baby, whose angry protests, which now included kicks as well as screams, had dislodged its coverings.

"Whose child is this, then?"

It had a somewhat lighter version of the same red hair as the woman.

"Hit's no mine, if that's what you're thinkin'. Or . . . 'tis mine and no mine. My sister's child; she died. Mr. Geddes or one of the old gossips, they did not tell you of this in June?"

He shook his head. "Oh, Isobel."

She shrugged. "Nivver mind her. What of my son? What has happened to my boy?"

His face reflected his distress. "I have been forbidden——"

She cut him off with a cry, a wail even louder than the infant's. "Have ye no heart?"

He had a heart; he also had a son and two daughters, and he looked with great pity upon the desperate woman. She thrust a small parcel at him.

"Will ye take this tae him?"

"How can . . . ?" He cleared his throat. "I won't be back at the Bay until late August, you know that."

"Can you no hide hid? 'Tis nothin' bad. 'Tis naught but wee stockins and a letter." She paused. "You could say your wife knit the stockins; you could do this for me."

He held out his hand and she thrust the parcel at him; he put it quickly in the deep right-hand pocket of his coat. Then he leant down and whispered something in her ear. She whirled around and disappeared into the noisy crowd.

"The rogue," he muttered. "The bastard!" Then he hurried along to where he could see the agent waiting for him outside his office.

"Captain Hanwell."

"Mr. Geddes."

"A good journey?"

"Tolerably so, thank you. Mr. Wishart is just behind me with the mail."

They went in together and shut the door. There was much important business to discuss, but all afternoon he kept patting that right-hand pocket like a man who has put away his pipe yet wonders if it was well and truly out—or whether it might suddenly come to life and set his clothes on fire.

1862 STROMNESS, ORKNEY

"ALIVE AND WELL." These were the whispered words that kept Isobel going all those years, although they were said just once: "Alive and well."

"Dere," she wrote. *"O my Dere, the shippe is to goe to night so I give this pasel to the capn a good man so you may receeve hit safe.*

"Your Mother Till Death"

Sewed up the letter and the wee stockings and coolie: *"c/o Capn Hanwel for Albany Fort."*

For twenty years, the letters following more or less the same pattern, all the hurt and grief underneath the lines like rocks just below the water's surface; she had to negotiate around them or she was sunk. Expected, at first, a reply from me and I did write, I *did*, not knowing then the treachery of our honourable chief. I wrote the letters you never received, wrote them until he got rid of me as well, "sent away as unfit for this service."

The stockings grew longer with each passing year; she

observed the growing boys in the house next door, the boys in the street. Grabbed a leg, a foot, to measure against after first scrubbing it with a bit of wet rag, so that they escaped from the stoop with one pale leg, the other in its usual grimy state. Careful, so careful, when turning the little heel. Her hands, which had become used to axes and guns, ropes, the leather harnesses of dogs, struggled at first with the needles, the turning of heels. Not knowing that learning to work stockings for her son would become her livelihood, such as it was; that in the end sailors would give her a good price for her worsted stockings.

For twenty years, the annual parcel out, *c/o Capn Hanwel*, *c/o Capn Hanwel, Jr.* And then she gave up writing. She could not imagine him any longer. He was a man now and a gentleman; why would he want to acknowledge her? Was he even in Rupert's Land still, or did he live in England? Gave up writing, but did not give up hope.

"May God prosper and proteck you is the sincer wishe Dr Son of yore pore Mother doant for get we pore mothers farewell."

For twenty years, down to the ship for a letter or even a word from one of the men. They turned their heads away. Nothing. She might as well have thrown him in the sea. Surely someone had news of him? She approached Mr. Geddes, but he shook her off: "I know nothing of this—nothing." No doubt he was worried about the bills mounting up in his office. Bills from tailors and furniture-makers. The possibility of an action. It was put out, later, that he had been in "ill health" at this time. Such worries, and here was this woman with her wild red hair and dragging skirts! He'd had his orders and so he did nothing, nothing at all. Nor did his successor.

In 1810, a quiet nod one afternoon from Captain Hanwell and the whispered words: "Alive and well." Alive and well! She tried to kiss his hand, but he, too, shook her off (but gently) and hurried towards the agent's house.

"Alive and well." She lived on that for the rest of her life.

He held out his arms to her, but she ignored him.

"Ma! Ma!"

"Be a good boy, James," she said. "Think of me sometimes."

Tears blinding her so she would have stumbled and fallen if Magnus had not grabbed her firmly by the arm.

The sloop was waiting; there was a mist on the river (what had she done!). The high stockade with the sun coming up behind it (Ma! Ma!), the men in the boat turning away from her, on their way home now, money waiting for them at Mr. Geddes's office, enough to buy a small piece of land, perhaps. And she—unnatural woman— dismissed.

"This woman is no longer suitable."

Mary, her dark sister, holds the crying child, her child. How can she give him up? She stands and is about to leap over the side, but the men pull her down. "For God's sake, woman!"

A bend in the river and all is lost.

The captain gave her a closet off the galley to sleep in, to eat in. The men did not want to eat with her; the sailors considered her bad luck. The resentful cook, whose sleeping place she had usurped, left food for her outside the canvas curtain——lobscouce, skillygalee.

The cry of the gulls made her breasts leak.

She could neither eat nor sleep; how could she eat when her heart was broken? But Captain Hanwell heard of the uneaten meals and came to see her.

"You must eat," he said. "I'll have no unnecessary corpses on this ship." Then, quietly, "You did what you thought was best." Laid his large red hand upon her shoulder. "If you don't eat, if you sicken, I shall be blamed." He sent in, every night, a tot of brandy from his own store. Her breasts were caked with dried milk, her face was stiff with tears.

MY FATHER, MAGNUS INKSTER, for whom I was named, was minister in the parish of Orphir. He was a native of Orkney, but my mother was an in-comer from Aberdeen, where my father had studied for the ministry at Mareschal College. She was the younger sister of one of his fellow students, a good-looking, dark-haired woman whose name was Morag, but both my father and I called her Mother. (What he called her in their intimate moments, I don't know; it was obvious to anyone that they were well content with one another.) I was an only child, a lad with a weak chest, and so I was overprotected, especially by my mother, and I had very few playmates until the age of twelve. It was not that we saw ourselves as a cut above the people of the parish, even though my father was a learned man, for the minister's family ate much the same food as the tenant-farmer: porridge made from bere-meal, fish (dried or fresh), the occasional chicken, the inevitable kail. We had our own cow, named Curly-doddie because her breath in the spring-time smelt of wild clover, and so we did not lack for milk. Potatoes in season and bannock. Butcher meat only on hol-idays. Eggs. My father's payment for overlooking the spiri-tual lives of his parishioners was a smallish stipend and the rest "in kind." Both of my father's parents were dead (drowning and tuberculosis), and my maternal grandparents were in Aberdeen; there were uncles and aunts whom we saw occasionally, but when I look back I see, mostly, the bright circle—or triangle, if you will—of my father at one end of the table preparing his sermon and my mother and me at the other as I practised my sums or my reading.

I learned to read at a very early age and loved the Bible stories. Being small and sickly, I often imagined myself trans-formed into a David who would do some great deed and sur-prise everyone with my courage and daring. One thing I did notice: there didn't seem to be many only children in the Bible. Even wicked Cain had a brother—if only temporarily. Sometimes I longed for a younger brother, but when I read about Jacob and Esau, or Joseph and his brothers, or Ham, Shem or Japheth, or (worst of all) the sons of Adam, I con-soled myself with the scriptural evidence that perhaps it was no great loss to be without siblings. I don't really know why my parents had only one child; it was unusual. A dozen was more the case, or at the very least half a dozen. Indeed there was one minister, on Hoy, who had nineteen children. How that family managed I will never know. My mother loved children and taught the Sunday school, and I had, rather

jealously, watched my father caress the tops of small heads
as he passed. I had seen our rooster mount the hens and a
ram mount a ewe, but as a child I had no idea that men and
women did such things, and even when I found out, as all
young people do, with no help from their parents, I didn't
want to think about it. (Although from then on, one of my
great fears, as well as one of my great desires, was that I
would return home and find my mother with a baby in her
arms.) My mother would stand up and go to my father, lean
over his chair and smooth his fine hair back from his fore-
head with her long, capable fingers. I knew how good that
felt. Once I saw him reach up and touch her black curls,
murmur, "You have pagan hair," and laugh. There was no
doubt in my mind, later, that they were "one flesh." But I was
not the sort of child who asked bold questions, and so I
never knew why I was their only offspring.

When I was young I spent a great deal of time in my
father's company. I believe that he thought my mother cod-
dled me, and that a little taste of his company, away from the
manse, would be a good thing. (He who was *never* ill, *never*
had a winter cough for which he was subjected to mustard
plasters, my personal equivalent of the hair shirt.) Occasionally he took me with him when he visited parishioners, and
we often went out on great rambles. Like many parish ministers, he was something of an amateur naturalist, and he
taught me to see beauty in the smallest things—the yellow
lichen on a stone wall; the autumn light on the pewter-
coloured sea, where we might see a raft of eider ducks,
which we called, in our local dialect, dunters, or along the

shore the red-shanked waders called watery pleeps. We knelt down to gently examine the green-and-black stripes of a caterpillar, which, he told me, would one day be an emperor moth. We watched the hen harriers swoop down, searching the fields for their dinner, or leaned over high cliffs to observe the aaks, who balanced their eggs on their feet. The whole world was filled with wonder; even the smallest grootie-buckie shell carried within it a piece of God's grandeur. As we walked, he talked to me of the history of this place and told me tales of the Norsemen.

We often climbed Ward Hill, the highest point in Orphir, and as he waited for me to catch my breath (he who was never breathless) and stood staring out towards the Bay of Howton and beyond to the great inland sea called Scapa Flow, he would begin his tales of the brave men who came to these islands a thousand years ago in their great dragon-prowed ships, of how he and I were descended from these men. They were pagans, to be sure, at least until Earl Magnus, who was killed through treachery but later honoured by the great rose-coloured cathedral in Kirkwall that bore his name.

He told me of Odin and Thor; of Bragi; of Balder and Tyr, the god of war, one-handed because he had helped to chain up the wolf Fenrir, who, if he got loose, would bring about the end of the world.

I never tired of these stories and he never tired of telling them, although he was careful to add, each time, in a firm tone, "These are only fables, you know. None of this is true." I nodded solemnly and knew better than to ask why they seemed so much more interesting, or equally as interesting, as the boy Jesus chasing the moneylenders from the Temple (if only he'd had a sword!) or Moses bringing down the Ten Commandments.

On our way home, we picked wildflowers for my mother, buttercups and bog cotton and clover and the yellow iris we call seggies. Mother always received these offerings with delight and found a small pot or pitcher in which to display them.

I loved my mother with a kind of passive love, perhaps even a smug love, the young prince secure in the love of his servant, but I loved my father with all my heart. He was a tall, round-faced, merry-faced man with a halo of wispy hair; I thought he looked like the man in the moon. His family was an old one, brought to reduced circumstances in the days of the old odal system of inheritance (all must inherit equally, so all inherit little), but he never complained—as did some of his uncles and aunts, his sisters and brothers. He always seemed to me perfectly satisfied with his vocation (I suspect he saw it as the running of a good and productive farm), his wife and his only son. When I think of the word "contentment," I think of my father. He was the most contented person I have ever met. My mother was a worrier; worriers can never be completely content, because they do not live in the present.

One day, when I was eight years old, he received a message, carried to our house by a dirty, breathless, barefoot boy, not much older than I was, who looked me up and down in a scornful manner, full of his own gasping self-importance. "Please, sir, the Kirkwall doctor needs you. He be comin' in his cart."

My father had promised me an afternoon walk, and I looked at him in distress. *Promises*, said my eyes; promises were sacred in our family. He shook his head. "Tomorrow," he said as he put on his coat.

"I want to come with you," I said.

Did he take me because he thought he was going to the bedside of some old man or woman, and he felt it was time I was shown the face of death? Was that why there was no real objection from my mother? I saw a look pass between them. "If necessary," he said, "the boy can stay in the cart."

The doctor was my father's closest friend, not so learned as he, for at the time the doctor qualified a medical degree was something of a joke and could often be purchased with the right money and connections, and the doctor's father had been a well-to-do merchant in Kirkwall. Mostly he relied on nostrums he made up himself, and when, on occasion, he had to resort to surgery, not all his patients died. What endeared him to my father was his willingness to visit the poor; he often paid for their cordials and such out of his own pocket. The only time I didn't like him was when he bled me.

He didn't notice me at first, he was in such a state of agitation. "Magnus," he said, "I think this is going to be a bad business. I'm truly sorry to call you away, but I need help."

"What is it?"

"I'm not sure, but a woman at Neverholme Farm has gone mad and I've been sent for." Just then he became aware of my presence. "The boy here? Oh, no, no. He will have to go back to the manse."

My father hesitated. I had just recovered from yet another bout of bronchitis; already it would be a fair walk home, for we had set out on foot in order to meet up with the doctor as soon as possible, and I was slightly wheezy from my attempts to keep up with my father.

"I think he'd best come with us," my father said, frowning a little. "But he shall bide in the yard."

By now I had a lively and morbid curiosity. I wanted to see the madwoman so long as she didn't bite. I assumed that mad people, like mad dogs, like the wolf Fenrir, would want to bite you if they could. And what if she went for my father or the doctor? My father had his walking stick; perhaps he could fight her off with that? I did not want my father, like the god Tyr, to lose his hand.

We went a long way before we came to the farm and a scattering of miserable cottages. A woman and a group of children were standing outside. Our guide, the boy who had brought the message, jumped down immediately.

"Come quick, come quick," the woman said. "She's in the byre."

The doctor and my father jumped down, and when I saw that the children were going to follow them, I jumped down as well. I knew the doctor's horse would never run away; he was used to waiting patiently outside strange dwellings.

As there was only one outside door, we rushed through the main part of the house to get to the byre. I'd been in cottages like this a few times before and the fuggis of the peat and human and animal bodies made me gasp and stung at my eyes. Most of the poor farm-folk went around red-eyed and slightly weeping, for there were no windows in such places, only the lum in the roof to let out smoke and let in light. And there was another smell I couldn't place. It reminded me of the time my father lit a spill and the thing flared up, singeing his eyebrows and the front of his hair. Like that, only worse.

She was at the far end of the byre, huddled against the wall with one arm flung across her eyes as though there was too much light even in that dark place. The dog was lapping up something at the edge of her skirts.

"She's got a knife," said the other woman, who was standing well away.

"I don't think," said my father, "she wishes harm to anyone except herself." He and the doctor stepped forward at the same time.

"Mrs. Gunn," said the doctor, "you must come with me now."

My father touched her arm.

"Mrs. Gunn, will you no give me the knife?"

For a few moments no one moved, no one made a sound except the cow stamping nervously in its stone stall. We could hear its worried snorts and sniffles. I could hear my heart pounding in my ears.

"Gie it o'er, lass," said my father, touching her arm again. Without taking her arm from across her eyes, she reached into her skirts with the other. We all drew back, except my father and the doctor.

"That's right," he said. "That's all right." She handed my father the knife, and he nodded and beckoned to the other woman.

"Will you put this back where it belongs?" And turning to the children, not realizing that I had disobeyed him and was one of them, he commanded us to leave.

We ran back through the house and outside to wait and see what would happen next. The others spoke not a word to me or to each other. There was a boy of about thirteen and the neighbour boy who had come to fetch us and some girls, one almost a woman. The youngest child looked to me about three or four; she was the only one with red hair. She was sucking her fingers and staring at nothing at all. Not a pretty child and very dirty. Not the sort of little sister I dreamt of having.

When they led the mother out, my father on one side, the doctor on the other, her hands were bound behind her back with old rags. The hands were covered in blood and the back of her skirt was dark with it.

"Where is your father?" the doctor asked the thirteen-year-old.

"Awa' tae th' peats."

"You must go and get him, then. Tell him we have taken your mother away."

The grieve's wife, for that was the other woman, agreed to stay on for a while, but she couldn't stop all night. The older girls would have to cope; they nodded.

The woman was placed in the cart, and then, while my father and I waited with her, the doctor went back inside and came out with a small bundle. He muttered something and picked up the reins.

I looked back at the children. They still had not moved or spoken, except for the boy, whom I could see running across the fields towards the shore. The littlest child still sucked on her fingers, staring and staring.

The mother did not look back, nor did they call out to her. She was somewhere else now, in another place where she could neither hear nor see them.

The doctor dropped us off at the bottom of our road. He had given the woman something and now she was asleep, covered up with an old blanket. My father paused.

"Are you sure you can manage the rest of this?"

"I'm sure."

"Poor woman, poor lassie."

"Aye."

"Where is he taking her?" I said to my father as we walked along.

"To gaol."

I nodded. She had done something dreadful, although I wasn't exactly sure what. She had to be punished. "Is she one of the damned?" I asked.

He didn't answer, but suddenly leaned down and gave me such a hug that he knocked the breath from me. "Hush," he said. "Hush."

When we resumed walking, he said, "I would like it if you said nothing of this to your mother. I will tell her, of course—there are no secrets between us—but I'd rather you said nothing."

"If she asks me . . . ?"

"She won't."

Nor did I tell her. I knew better, knew that in my father's version there would be certain omissions, that I could get my father in trouble if I revealed all that I had seen. She might not trust him to take me out again. As it happened, I was washed and put to bed right after tea because she thought I was looking pale. I said my prayers and then got into bed; she kissed me and took away the lamp.

From my room I could hear the murmur of voices and— could it be?—the sound of my father weeping. Somehow that upset me more than anything else that day. I felt helpless, for I did not know how I could comfort him. I thought that I would never get to sleep, or that once asleep I would have nightmares (I was prone to nightmares). But perhaps there was a sleeping draught in my milky tea, for the next thing I knew it was morning. Nevertheless, in my waking hours what I had seen haunted me; it haunts me still.

It was Isobel, years later, who told me what I'd guessed and told me why.

"Hid was another wee girl," she said, "and me mother threw hid in the fire."

ISOBEL WAS SUPPOSED TO be the last child. When the drunken father came stumbling in, the child, minutes old, was lifted—no, yanked—from her mother's arms. He opened the swaddle of clean cloths, so old they were as soft as silk, holding her up by one great dirt-encrusted hand and pulling her legs apart. Even in the dim light of the oily cruisie he could see—or not see—that what he was seeking, a small boy's whirlygigger, wasn't there. He gave a loud bark and threw the child down as roughly as he had drawn her up, then stumbled out into the dark night.

Could her body remember what she herself could not, had been told only by her older sisters? The callused hand forcing her legs apart, the shout of disappointment that set the hens to squawking and the new lamb to bleating for its mother. And after he left, her mother's weak tears falling on her head and the neighbour women, who were sitting up all night to ward off the peerie folk, patting and comforting, "Shh, shh, dinna fash thyself. Hush." And from the pocket of one, the borrowed sixpence brought out and placed in the spoon, the spoon dipped in ale and offered to the babe, as was the old custom, for the first sup must be from silver.

The brother had been sent out long before, to sleep in the byre or wherever he chose that night, but the sisters watched from corners while the hens clucked and the new lamb cried for its mother. The baby, soothed by the spirits, fell asleep against her mother's freckled breast. Another wee girl, and more than enough of them already.

She was named Isobel, after the mother. She, the last shake of the bag—except for the one who died later—and then the mother was taken away.

Had he done it to her then? Willed her, by his rough contempt in the first hour of her life, to wish she were a boy? What good was the knife in the bed, the borrowed Bible, the neighbour women sitting up, when the threat was from another quarter, closer to home? Humans can do damage greater than any fairy folk.

Holding her up to the lamp, gawking in disbelief, spreading her legs. Nothing. Another daughter!

Did her mother lie awake that night, straight and stiff as a plank, the dark blood leaking out of one end and the tears dropping down from the other? The child had her mother's dark red hair and soon her mother's name, but their destinies were so very different, or so I thought until tonight, as I sit up with the corpse of the first woman I cared for, save my own dear mother, waiting for a knock upon the door.

They're all dead now, except the boy, and God knows where he's at. He could be dead as well, a boy no longer but a man over fifty, a middle-aged man struck down by any number of ailments. And I won't be far behind. At the last census, seven women and one man in their eighth decade in the town of Stromness. Now six women, and I am only passing through. We're a hardy lot, but few live to extreme old age and many die young. The sea claims us, or tuberculosis, or—in the old days—the smallpox. Poverty, that too. That Isobel Gunn lived as long as she did, given the way she lived in her last years, I put down only to a fierce belief that before she died she would see her son once more. Well, she was mistaken. I put advertisements in the *Scotsman*, the London *Times*, the Toronto *Globe*, even the paper in Sydney, although my letter will not yet have arrived in Australia and now she's dead. Nothing. The "Honourable Gentlemen" in London know, I'm certain of that, but their collective lips have been sealed for half a century. They maintain that he died shortly after he was removed to Fort Garry. I don't believe it, but there's nothing more I can do, an old man and soon in my grave myself. A strange business, and myself only in near the beginning and near the end. Not exactly a witness, but I probably know more about Isobel Gunn than anyone else alive. I need to set down what I know for a fact and what she told me and what I can only speculate upon. The human mind is a mystery; why do any of us do the things we do? Trained for a church I no longer believe in, I suppose I should say God wills it. Whatever happens to us, good or ill, we must accept it as the will of God.

If that is the case, then God is the schoolyard bully, as well as the self-important dominie with the cane. How seldom is God the gentle hand upon the brow! I have always had great difficulty with God, that stern God of our church. Surely such a Creator would have sent down someone more like Mars than gentle Jesus? Naturally, except when debating among friends, I keep these views to myself. It wasn't so long ago that they burned witches here, and the belief in devils, large and small, has never died away. Signs, portents, lucky days and times of the month. Even now, in the enlightened year of our Lord 1862, no self-respecting bride would wish to marry other than on "the gruein mune," and no one would sleep with his head towards the door, for that is the way that corpses lie. Yes, my dear, I have done that for you, and I shall sit up the eight nights, have already sat up three—a woman's task, but I wanted it. The neighbours wish you gone, but I'll not have it until the proper time. Even the local doctor, holding his handkerchief to his nose, anticipating smell, although there is none. I sit wrapped in shawls, with the window only slightly open, the sea tang blowing in. At least with the dark there are no more children outside peering in, but here inside I have been extravagant with candles, can hear the ghost of the chief factor lecturing me, handing over the three bundles wrapped in blue paper: "Eighteen pounds of candles, Mr. Inkster, that is your lot—the same for everyone. Being learned and a schoolmaster, you are no doubt fond of reading. Husband your allotment, Mr. Inkster, husband it—or you will find yourself without, long before the ship comes back again."

The draughts make the lights cast dancing shadows on the walls, as though all the ghosts of our past attend us, but I am not afraid of the dead. I would welcome them tonight if I knew how to call them up—my dear mother and father, the doctor, my own dear wife, even Mr. Morton and the rest of the men at Albany Fort, Nellie, Isobel herself, James, if he is indeed dead. James most particularly, for there are questions I wish to ask. That is what really haunts me this night, the question of James. Would his spirit come to wait upon his mother on her last nights above the ground? Could he tell us what happened to him? Was he happy? Did he remember his mother at all? Did he remember me? Am I sitting up these nights not solely out of respect for Isobel, but also because I am waiting for him to appear, living or dead, in one form or another? This landscape lends itself to superstition, with standing stones and burial mounds and skulls turned up in farmers' fields. A history of Viking raids and violence. We need all the luck we can manufacture.

As I have said, Isobel was supposed to be the last child.
No more, if they were all going to turn out girls—the one
son, George, being a fluke. The family was poor—tenant
farmers of the very poorest sort—on land whose chief crop
seemed to be stones. Boys, strong boys who could help at
home and hire themselves out to the fishermen or the laird
in certain seasons, were what was wanted. It was not that
the women worked less, but that they were paid less—that
was the problem. I used to see those women, in the time of
kelp-gathering, with the great baskets we call caisies fastened by a strap to their backs, barefoot, feet mottled with
cold, fingers swollen like cows' udders and the seawater
from the tangle soaking their heavy clothes. Or a woman
yoked to two ten-gallon pails of water, picking her way over
the stones, barefoot again, heading home from the well.
Beasts of burden, and not much chance of any improve-
ments in their lifetime. Were they God-fearing? Oh, yes,
especially the fear part. That's why the only conclusion that
could be drawn, even if the evidence hadn't been staring us
in the face, was that the poor mother had lost her mind.
Isobel was supposed to be the last child, and the mother was
banished to sleep with her girls while George, the son, took
her place in the neuk-bed with his father. But however it
happened, the mother Isobel was pregnant again when the
child Isobel had just turned four. The father was a man in the
prime of life—no doubt drink and the devil did the rest.
The results of this pregnancy changed many lives, including
my own.

I did not see Isobel again for several years. After the

mother's death, none of the Gunns attended services, not even on the great days in the Christian calendar. And at the age of twelve I was sent off to Stromness Academy, part of my fees being paid by my father's friend the doctor. I was sent to board with the Reverend Mr. Clouston and his family.

Although I was bright, precocious even, and loved learning, my time in Stromness was not a happy one. At the Cloustons' I was treated as an ordinary boy, just one of several, not a delicate, indulged, only child. Why had I ever for a moment wanted siblings, especially brothers? Because things were so strict at their home (much more so than at the manse at Orphir), the Clouston boys were absolute demons in the schoolyard. Anyone weaker, and I was definitely weaker, was fair game. They pummelled me and tripped me up and once made me eat a worm. The girls weren't much better; they made up rhymes and laughed at me. I can hear them still:

> Magnus Noddie puir auld body
> Knocked his head on a curlie-doddie
> Up he got, doon he fell
> Knocked his head on a tattie-bell.

Although they were required to "speak properly" in the house, once outside they reverted to the local dialect and the sneering tones of the poorer children in the town.

Neither the schoolmaster nor the schoolmistress had any control in the schoolyard. Besides, they were both afraid of the reverend and his wife, who had great influence in the town and no doubt could have had them dismissed in an instant.

And the manse itself was cold in every sense. No fires before November and endless reading of the Bible in the evenings, especially St. Paul. It seemed a different book altogether when read out by the Reverend Mr. Clouston, a tall, thin, hwinckle-faced man who seemed absolutely devoid of humour. Mrs. Clouston scrubbed and polished, scrubbed and polished. She did our faces as though we had no more nerve endings than the stone sink or a wooden cog. Since she was so obviously one of the saved, why did she have to work so hard? And her sighs at the sinfulness of the world! Sighs so loud they must have been heard in heaven. I longed for my father and mother, and at half-term, when my father came to fetch me for a few days, I began to weep as soon as I was in the door (for I wasn't stupid, and waited until I had my mother present) and announced that I wasn't going back. I exaggerated— but not much—the coldness of the Clouston home and the terrors of the schoolyard. Yet somehow my mother was not on my side this time, although I was spoiled while I was at home and they concentrated their collective attention on me, making me feel once again loved and wanted and special. (I thought of myself as special, with my weak chest and strong intelligence—hadn't the master said I could read as well as he?) They ignored my tears and sent me back again.

As we stood at the Cloustons' door, my father said quietly, "Be a brave soldier." A Christian soldier, I assumed he meant. He believed strongly in education, and if I had to be separated from my family to achieve that end, so be it. And there was another thing, but I did not know it until later: my mother was slowly dying of some internal complication. By the summer holidays, she would be dead.

I look back on that boy now, and although I can acknowledge that his distress was great and feel some sympathy, I can only applaud my parents' stand. I was rapidly turning into a physical and moral coward and a prig. Like a fledgling shoved out of the nest, it was time I learned to fly.

My sweet mother told me, in her last days, that mine was not the only pillow wet with tears.

Stromness then was nothing like it is now, just one long sinuous street and a permanent population of perhaps five hundred souls. The street was so narrow in one place that if two portly men approached each other at the same time, one would have to flatten himself against the wall of a house or back up into a close. Kirkwall was "the metropolis," with its cathedral and gentlefolk, but for a lad from Orphir, Stromness itself, especially the harbour, was magical. No one in Orkney lives very far from the sea. The sea is, and always has been, the central fact in our lives. Even my father's sermons were full of references to the sea around us. And Stromness, particularly during the Napoleonic Wars, was a bustling port. The English Channel was unsafe, and ships preferred to come up the east side of Britain and out into the Atlantic through the Pentland Firth. Sailors and fishermen and the merchant ships and the ships of the Royal Navy, not to mention the ships going out and coming back from Hudson Bay or Greenland or the Davis Strait—all this fed my romantic soul, even though I knew that a life upon the

sea, in whatever capacity, from lowly fisherman to captain of
an ocean-going vessel, was hard and dangerous. On Saturday
afternoons most of the boys headed for the harbour to watch
the fishermen mend their nets or caulk their boats, or to
stare at the captain and crew of the big ships when they were
in port. The ships of the Hudson's Bay Company were particularly fascinating to us because they went to Rupert's
Land, to the New World, where there were wild Indians and
bears. None of us, although in and out of the water all
summer long, had even been across the Firth to mainland
Scotland, yet we talked knowledgeably of capstans and rat-
lines and shrouds and binnacles—boys whose biggest journey so far was to Lammas Fair in Kirkwall! Why, we called
this island, our biggest island, "Mainland." It was hard to
imagine some place as far away as Rupert's Land; those who
had been there and returned (and there were many, from just
about every parish in Orkney) seemed to us like men who
had been to the moon.

  We were, of course, told to stay away from the men who
gathered at the harbour, these rough men with their earrings
and tattoos and foul language, but that just added to the
attraction. We secretly repeated snatches of songs we heard
the sailors sing—of the cruel sea, of women left behind, of a
place called Ratcliffe Highway, of drink and press gangs and
the loss of gold or life. We listened to all this and then went
back to our God-fearing dwelling-places, said our prayers
before meals and at bedtime and dreamt extravagant dreams.
I felt that it was my Viking soul that responded to the call of
the sea, but I do not know of a boy anywhere who is not

attracted to water—unless it is used for washing hands and faces. Mrs. Clouston gave her great sighs, but she couldn't keep us away from the harbour and its delights.

When I was fifteen, it was suggested by the headmaster that I begin my university studies, for from an early age it had been understood that I was destined, like the apostles, to be a fisher of men, not of any other of God's creatures. My father's friend the doctor had matriculated at St. Andrews University, not far from Edinburgh, and so persuasive a champion was he that it was arranged (again with financial help from his family, for he was my godfather and had only one daughter, no sons) that I be sent to the United College of St. Leonard and St. Salvator to begin an arts course leading to the degree of Master of Arts. After that, if all went well, I would enter St. Mary's College to pursue my theological preparation for the ministry. And after that, I would emerge from Divinity Hall, as it tended to be known, and would undergo the process of licensing as a preacher. For this I would be examined orally on church doctrine and would give a series of trial sermons before the presbytery under whose jurisdiction I normally lived—in my case, the presbytery covering the Orkney Isles.

My heart sank. Later, when I had my final falling-out with God and relied on Shakespeare, Dante and Bunyan to get me through my dark night of the soul, I came across, in *Macbeth*, the words—it is Banquo who speaks them, in a scene with the witches—"What, will this line stretch out to the crack of doom?" Banquo speaks thus out of amazement and curiosity, but that spring day, when my father and the doctor and I went on a ramble along the cliffs to discuss my future, I felt as though my whole life had suddenly narrowed, almost as though I were being asked to reduce my future to a monk's robe and a single cell. I don't think it had ever dawned on me, until that day, how fast my future was approaching.

Leave Orkney? Study for years in a place hundreds of miles away that the doctor had always said was bitter with the wind off the North Sea? Be separated from my beloved father, who had clung to me—we had clung to each other—and wept like a child the night my mother died? How would he manage without me? He had a housekeeper now, a widow who came in daily to cook and tidy, but I knew how much he relied on my visits and my almost daily letters. I looked at him with tears in my eyes; I would never be so robust as he, but I was now nearly as tall. He tried to smile.

"You've been given the great gift of a lively and enquiring mind," he said. "Such gifts must be used, not wasted. You will do splendidly, I know that."

"Then why not Aberdeen?" I said. "It's your old school, it's closer."

"Our friend the doctor thinks you will suit St. Andrews better." They exchanged one of those adult looks that I had not yet learned to read. Now I think it had something to do with my mother's family, who had never been happy that she had married an Orkneyman who lured her away to that strange, backward place.

And so it was settled and we continued our walk. In the late-afternoon light I was once again intensely aware of how beautiful my homeland was, a fierce beauty to be sure, but a beauty I was used to. The high cliffs with the boiling sea below, the purple heather and the lichen-covered stones, the strange light, so clear it was like a draught of cool water. I grew more and more melancholy; I, who had longed for adventure, suddenly wanted never to go anywhere at all.

Then, just as we were about to turn back, we came across some rope-walkers, a not unusual sight, and stopped to watch. Birds' eggs have always been a traditional way to supplement the meagre diet of the poor folk, and many men and boys brave the cliffs and the screaming seabirds, allowing themselves to be lowered on ropes towards the nests. My father had done this when he was young.

Someone was down there now, and several young people lay flat on their bellies, holding on to the thick rope and waiting for the signal to pull the brave thief up.

"There 'tis!" called one to the others. "Pull her up the noo!"

The pulling-up was a slow and delicate business, for the rope-walker, forty feet above the sea, had to fight off the angry birds with a stick and still protect the eggs, which he carried in a kind of sling. His stick also served to keep him from banging into the side of the cliff. It was a tricky thing all round. Just a month before, a boy had fallen headfirst to his death upon the rocks. Only the bravest men and boys undertook it.

So I was surprised to see, as the face and the whole form of the rope-walker appeared at the edge and then up and over the cliffside, the eggs having been handed up first, that the boy was actually a girl, a red-headed girl whose face I thought I knew. I wasn't sure, because one side of her face had been badly disfigured by smallpox, but it had to be the same girl who had stood, sucking her fingers, as my father and the doctor led her mad mother away.

My father recognized her too, and gave a small "Oh" of surprise.

She was dressed as a boy and most of her hair was tucked under the kind of tam-o'-shanter the boys wore on Sundays, but some had come loose and she swiped at it with her free hand.

The young people ignored us completely, examined the eggs and then carefully wrapped them up in the cloth that had served as a sling. They set off across the fields towards their farm without a word to us, although it was obvious from their glance that they knew the doctor.

"Isn't that . . . ?" said my father.

"Aye. The Gunns. They survive, God knows how. The father is a drunken sot, but between George and the older girls they manage to plough the field when it's time to sow or hire themselves out for the kelp-gathering and labour at whatever comes to hand. The oldest girl, Jannet, is in service in Kirkwall." He sighed. "Amazing, really. There's a fierce pride in there somewhere, although that Isobel is a terror."

We had now turned back, and the two men talked as we went along. Isobel—so that was her name.

"A terror? How so?"

"She dresses as a lad, refuses to learn her letters, has suffered more broken limbs in her young lifetime than the rest of that family put together."

"Has obviously been visited by the smallpox as well. But not the others?"

"They all had it. Ach! The grieve's family came down with it, and before I knew about it that stupid woman had given the Gunns some bannock smeared with the pustules. She thought it was a kind of variolation, I suppose; she's not the only one who has this idea. Of course, once they'd et the bannock they were 'safe.' They caught smallpox from the grieve's children, and Isobel nearly died. They could have had the new vaccine, but oh, no—superstitious fools."

I had had the vaccine, as had my father and mother, who had a round white mark the size of a shilling on her thigh. When I was very small she told me it meant she had been to the moon. Mine was smaller and on my upper arm, as was my father's.

"What will become of that family—those Gunns?" I was surprised at myself for asking.

"I don't know, laddie. I suppose they'll go on living at Neverholme Farm until the landlord evicts them. George is a good lad, and with the surfeit of women around here I suspect at least one of the girls—probably Isobel—will remain a spinster and look after her father until he dies. It's George I feel most sorry for; he told me once he wanted to go to the Bay, but I canna see that happening. Ah, well—life is hard for some and that's the truth."

Nothing was said about the mother, and I didn't ask.

In October I left, and although I did not know it at the time, I was not to return to Orkney for six long years. I did not see Isobel Gunn again until I landed, in 1808, at the bottom of the Bay, a grown man, at least in form, full of questions about who I was and what I had been put on this earth to do. But I am getting ahead of myself and this is meant to be Isobel's tale, not mine—or as much hers as mine. So I'll leave my father and the doctor and myself up there on the cliffs of Orphir, hurrying a bit now, for dark clouds had come up and covered the sun. We wanted to be home before they released their rain.

GEORGE GUNN TOOK OVER his father's duties as the man sank deeper and deeper into drink and despair. He had terrible nightmares in which he bellowed like a bull and cried out that all the devils in hell were after him. The winters were the worst, with the harvesting finished, the kelpmaking at an end and the fish dried or drying above the fire. They did not live in squalor—the girls saw to that—but they lived in a kind of spiritual poverty that must have been just as bad. It is true that man cannot live by bread alone—the soul must be nourished as well. The darkness of that wretched cot, with soot dripping down the walls and into their porridge and down their backs, and the daylight just a grey smudge in the hole in the roof, made them sullen towards the outside world and towards one another. *Wanhope*: a word I learned when reading over a set text in Old English. *Wan-hope* meant "despair."

Their cow died, and so for a long time there was ale on the porridge instead of milk, a not uncommon mixture in hard times. Isobel's prowess at rope-walking provided the only luxuries they ever had. Jannet, the sister in service in Kirkwall—according to Isobel, she was the prettiest of the girls and the quickest—soon became a trusted servant in the Baikie house, where she was employed. Twice a year she returned to the farm, bringing old clothes that had been given her and a few treats she had managed to buy with her savings: a cheese, a bit of butter, a few apples. She told them stories about the rich. The one Isobel remembered all her life was the time Jannet and the parlourmaid had listened at the door while Mrs. Baikie was entertaining a visitor to breakfast. They were having a bet as to who could get rid of fifty pounds the quickest. The maid had just gone in to clear when Mrs. Baikie buttered a piece of bread, placed the fifty-pound note on top and et it! The maid rushed back through the kitchen door, nearly knocking Jannet off her feet, she was so aghast. Fifty pounds. Seventeen years of hard work, nearly, and the woman swallowed it down like a sliver of cheese on toast.

They sat in the stinging dark of their cottage and couldn't take it in. Jannet thought it was comical—so out of her ken—but George was very angry. He called them all names and swore and made Jannet cry. She said she wouldn't come again, but her sisters ran after her and begged her not to mind. It *was* a wicked thing to do, was it not?

"I think," said Isobel to me, "that for Jannet, hid was like somethin' in a book."

"Not real."

"Aye. That's why she laughed. Hid wasna real."

The other girls left—for Kirkwall, Stromness, a neigh-bouring farm. Soon there were only the drunken father, George, Margaret (the middle sister) and Isobel.

At first, Isobel became a boy because she had to. She was very strong and could lift anything, *do* anything, her brother could. She guided the slanted plough that did not much more than scratch the surface of the ground. She planted oats and bere; she yoked herself to the harrow. Margaret tended the chickens, the kail-yard and the house; she made their coarse clothes. They went barefoot most of the year and in winter wore rivens of wrapped skins around their feet. The father lay on his bed and cursed or sat on a plank-bench and cursed. He could see the disgust in his children's eyes.

Once a fortnight George, who had so roundly damned the gentlefolk of Kirkwall, set out at dusk, his lantern a candle stuck in a sheep's skull, and took the long, long walk to town, ostensibly to see his two sisters who were in service there, but also to visit the alehouses and participate, however briefly, in the company of men. He always returned, for he knew their bit of the farm would go under without him.

For a long time Isobel accepted her life's lot. Margaret was not strong, so the youngest daughter would be the female guardian of her father's old age. Unless he died, and there were many nights she wished he would. She never thought she would have a man of her own, and when the sis-ters got together and pulled the kail-runts, counting the buds to see how many babies they would bring forth, she just laughed at them, daft lassies. Who wanted babies? All that shite and dribble and greetin.

Refused to tie her hair up in the virgin's ribbon, but let it hang wide and loose or wore it in a single plait, down her back, like a sailor.

Isobel did not have a reflective nature, but over the months, as she told me her life story, I began to see that she felt what the others did not: that her mother's act, so hideous, so unnatural, had branded the youngest daughter forever an outcast from the world of women. There were many women with faces marked by smallpox who went on to marry; and although the one side of her face was severely scarred, as though pecked at by a bird, the other side, for some strange reason, was almost unmarked. No, what set her apart was her mother's crime. It was as though what the mother had done—the mother with the same name, her name—had pitted and pocked her soul the way the disease had damaged her body. Does that sound fanciful? *I* never got over the sight of that woman in the byre, her arm flung across her eyes, the dog licking the blood from around her skirts, the bundle of the dead baby, the blank faces of the children, especially the youngest, the one with the hair like dark flame. And it wasn't my mother. It was nothing to do with me; I was only a terrified witness. And yet, I think I was damaged too. If Isobel was somehow spiritually stricken that afternoon, then so was I.

JANNET BEGAN WALKING out with a young tailor named John Craig, and through him, on one of his visits to Kirkwall,

Isobel's brother met a man called John Scarth, Craig's friend. Scarth was a slightly older man who had spent years in Rupert's Land, working for the Hudson's Bay Company. George and John Scarth became great alehouse friends, and Isobel's brother began to bring home tales much more interesting than Jannet's stories of what the well-to-do burghers of Kirkwall ate and drank and wore. One day George brought home the tale-teller himself.

John Scarth had signed on again for another tour at the Bay and was waiting to be called back to Stromness and the ship. Meanwhile, he had a week or so to spare and had offered to help George with the repair of the byre and the thecking of a new roof. Margaret was not happy to see him. How were they to feed this extra mouth? Where was he to sleep?

John Scarth laughed. He had small, even teeth, very white, almost like milk teeth; he was small all round, small and wiry and dark. He said he had brought enough meal for himself and some left over, and it would be grand to sleep outside under the stars.

"We canna pay you," Margaret said.

"I'm no askin' for money."

"Then you're a fool," she said, and from then on shut her ears to him.

Not so Isobel and George. After the father had been put to bed and Margaret had retired to a corner with the lamp, knitting or mending or just sitting, waiting until the men went out and she and Isobel could go to bed, John Scarth told stories of his life in Rupert's Land.

I imagine her, Isobel, sitting there, a little ways off perhaps (she was, after all, an unmarried daughter of the house,
not a son), listening in the dark. There is a special potency to
stories told in the dark. He was a grand talker, she said, and
in that dank and foetid cottage he created pictures of a world
of intrepid men, of daring and risk-taking and plenty to eat:
partridges and ptarmigan and pork sent out from England.
Fish and hare. Hard work and camaraderie. The Canadians
who spoke French and canoed for miles up and down the
rivers and worked for the North West Company, fierce rivals
for the beaver pelts and other furs upon which the fortunes
of the Hudson's Bay Company depended. "We call them
mangeurs du lard," he said. "They call us oafish oatmeal eaters."
Isobel did not know what the first phrase meant, but from
Scarth's smile she gathered it was an equal insult. "But there's
no real trouble between us," he added. "We're friendly rivals,
you might say." The winters of ice and snow, snowshoes and
sledges. And at the end of it all, most of your wages intact,
held by Mr. Geddes, to be paid out on your return to
Orkney.

Good wages. Clothes. Food. Adventure.

One night he talked of snow blindness and how he himself, sent on a trek to Fort Churchill way up north in the Bay,
alone with only his pack and his dog, became lost and then
blind from the glare of the snow. For thirty days he stumbled
along, praying he was heading in the right direction. When
his supplies were exhausted, he ate the inside of the bark of
trees. He dug down in the snow until he felt the lichen growing on the rocks; he ate that. His dog died of starvation and

he ate the dog. He had eaten one of his shoes and was ready to give up when a hunting party found him and led him to the fort. He lost all but the big toe on that one foot from the frostbite. And his eyes stung so—it was like having sand rubbed into his eyelids. Only hot water, as hot as you could stand it, cured the snow blindness.

He told all this in such a cheerful tone that Isobel was both appalled and excited. She could see him, John Scarth, in his coat he called a capote and his big fur mitts, striding across the snow with his dog. The solitary figure in the vast landscape. She shut her eyes and imagined being snow-blind. She could imagine stinging eyes; here in this house her eyes stung always from the smoke. Sinking up to the knees in snow, for he had, in the end, eaten even the leather thongs of the snowshoes and thrown away the wood. Having tried in his blindness to light a fire with flint and a bit of moss, blowing, blowing, he had caught his beard on fire instead and burnt his chin.

Just the crossing would be enough, she thought. Icebergs as big as barns, polar bears, Eskimos in their skin boats. He showed George a carving of a seal and her pup made from walrus ivory, a beautiful thing; he beckoned Margaret and Isobel to come and see. Tempted out of her corner, Margaret held the cruisie so they could have a good look. White. Smooth. They touched it hesitantly with their rough hands that were never quite clean.

"Give them some molasses and ship's biscuit," John said (smiling his smooth, white smile), "and they'll trade you anything."

I doubt John Scarth had any idea of the effect of his words on Isobel Gunn. After this week, he would never see her again. But George, a big, husky fellow like George. He must have had thoughts about George. The Company could do with men like George. A bit old to be starting out, but still.

Isobel lay sleepless beside her older sister. No women were allowed at the factories, as he called these forts. It wasn't a place for women, he said. The life was too hard, and they'd just get in the way.

"No women at all?" George gave John Scarth a puzzled smile and the visitor smiled back.

"Lots of Native women. Country wives." He threw back his head and laughed. "Country marriages, we call them. Lots of children running around. No white women, is what I meant. Plenty of the other kind."

"And you?" George asked. "Do you have one of these country wives?"

John Scarth smiled his white smile but did not reply.

Isobel knew that George would never go. He had begun courting one of the grieve's daughters, and besides, he was much too loyal to leave his father and Margaret, who wasn't strong. Without him they would soon collapse; their tenancy would be taken from them and they would join the dozens of itinerant beggars who roamed the parishes. Even if Jannet helped and took them in—but how could she? After her marriage to John Craig she might keep her post at the Baikies', but she'd soon have babbies to look after and John Craig was only an apprentice tailor—they could not marry for at least a year.

She sat up in bed, ran her hands over her thin body, her small breasts. She was twenty-two years old; there was nothing to hold her here. She was tired of her father's curses and his vomit, weary of his pathetic tears. He wanted another son? Well, he would have one. But with a different name, and not from this parish.

By the time she heard the cock crow, she had made up her mind to go.

THROUGHOUT HER CHILDHOOD, Isobel had been haunted by her mother.

She came to her in dreams so real Isobel later thought of them as visions. Barefoot, her hair loose, sometimes she carried the burning babe, sometimes a dead lamb, its eyes pecked out by ravens. She smiled, but it was a terrible smile and in the distance could be seen the fires of hell. The very ground her mother walked on was burning. Her mother spoke to her, but never in a language Isobel could understand—just a series of sounds, with pauses in between.

Once, her mother was hanging by the neck from a tall tree, but she was not alone. From every tree in that strange wood a figure hung, swaying a little, all barefoot, all women.

She kept her dreams to herself.

"Once you were at the Bay," I asked, "did the dreams continue?"

"No," she said, "but I'll see her again in hell."

Because she was mad, they had not in fact hanged the

mother. Because she was quiet (she never spoke), after a while they let her help a bit around the gaol. One day she simply walked away and threw herself down the well. Like the boy falling off the cliff, Isobel thought, only she had wanted it, the water, the peace.

When Isobel told me this, I could not help seeing again the young Isobel being drawn up over the cliff, with eggs in a cloth sling, the birds shrieking around her (oh, even a mother bird knew how unnatural, dived and screamed and would gladly peck out your eyes). Her own mother deliberately discarding her young, smothering it and throwing it in the fire. Did she see her own wild face rushing up at her, for an instant, as she hit the water? If Isobel had been a boy, would any of this have happened?

The mother was buried quickly outside the churchyard. The family walked away and never went back. Jannet and her sisters dressed the sad corpse in her simple wedding dress, which had been put aside, as is the custom here, for her death-day. They pulled on the bride's white stockings, yellowed with age. They tucked a sprig of purple heather in her hands. But there was no wake; only the grieve's wife came to say how sorry she was that this had happened. From the looks she gave the father, they could see she thought it was his fault.

Apparently both my father and mother had been there. Where was I? Playing quietly at home, I suppose. They often left me alone, trusting me, if they had parish work to do together.

When Isobel told me about her mother, I thought about hell. Why did we always picture our spiritual punishment as fire? The great Tuscan poet understood the awfulness of ice, of frozen water. We Orkney people have understood that for centuries. In some strange way did Isobel—thrilling to the stories of ice floes and icebergs and the terror of ships being trapped between two icy mountains, ground to pieces with the ship's crew left to die in the frozen sea—did she court death by water? Was that the only way she could atone for her mother's sin?

It was probably nothing like that—she simply wanted to start a new life. We have all wished that, at one time or another. Most of us never see a way of doing so, or even if we do, we are pulled back into our habitual routine, not just by cowardice, but also by ties of duty and of love. Isobel did not feel these ties, or not strongly, not then. Can you blame her?

THE SHIP WAS TO SAIL ON the twenty-first of June. Isobel left quietly two nights before and made her way to Kirkwall. She could barely write her name, so she did not leave a note— and what would she have written it on? They had no books except an old Bible without covers. In a drunken rage, the father had torn out the first two books and fed them to the fire. This had damned him for sure and the rest would have followed, but George snatched it away and hid it some- where. She could have awakened her sister, but that way might lead to pleading or discovery. She was sorry for Margaret, but she had to save herself. Once safely in Rupert's Land she would send a message.

Jannet thought she was mad. Why would she want to do such a thing? "An' ye'll no be here for the wadding, Isobel, an' the wadding-walk an' the fiddle an' all." Her sister was tearful at the thought.

"Get me some men's trews," Isobel said, "old, and make me a moustache, Jannet. I *will* go. I'll no bide in that dreadful place a minnit more."

"They'll find you out."

Isobel shook her head.

"If you manage to get t' the ship, Isobel, an' they catch you out, they'll throw you overboard. Hid isn't a game yer playin'."

"I wat that wael." She undid her plait and her hair fell down around her shoulders.

"Yer hair, Isobel! Yer lovely hair."

"Cut it off. 'Twill grow again."

By the light of a candle, Jannet carefully cut off her sister's long hair. Then she snuck away to the scullery, where the lamps were waiting to have their chimneys cleaned in the morning. She brought back lampblack and soot on a rag and some old trousers from a basket for the Destitute Poor. Mrs. Baikie was one of the Kirkwall ladies who visited the poor.

While Isobel waited, she looked around the closet that had been Jannet's living space for five years. A small bed, a chanty beneath, an old chest in which to keep her belongings. A Bible. Some dried flowers—no doubt a posy from her sweetheart, John. A nail for her shawl, another for her bonnet. There was no window, and although it was Midsummer's Eve the next day, and outside the sleepless summer sun was already beginning to show itself, the room was dark and chill. How did her sister stay cheerful, creeping up each night from the warmth and light below to such a dismal place? There were other servants, for this was a grand house: a man and his wife who slept out in an annex, a governess who slept with the children and a cook who slept downstairs in a room off the kitchen.

When Jannet returned, she whispered that the cook had nearly awakened, but snorted and went back to sleep, no doubt thinking it was rats.

"I musna lose my place here, Isobel!"

Isobel had brought a bit of rope in case the trousers were too big around the waist, but they fit quite well. She had also brought along a loose smock of George's and her old tam-o'-shanter. Jannet, holding up the candle in her left hand, worked carefully on her sister's face. Then she stepped back and nodded. They sat on the edge of the bed for a moment, hands clasped. Isobel knew that Jannet, who had been more mother than sister, was silently weeping, but she could not think of that. She knew she would not be caught, at least not until after the ship had sailed. She must think only of speaking in a low voice and as seldom as possible. She must think of avoiding, at all costs, John Scarth. She had sewed herself a cloth sausage on a cord she wore around her waist, and had even made herself a kind of funnel, so that she could relieve herself standing up. These things had taken a great deal of thought, and she was proud of them. When she showed them to Jannet, it was the one time all night her sister laughed.

In a little while Jannet got up and led Isobel down the

back stairs and out through the garden. She kissed her hands and wept some more, then silently let her go. Should anyone happen to see, they would just think it was the pretty servant with her sweetheart. At the last minute she thrust a small parcel into Isobel's hands.

"A small quantity," she whispered, "every month. Mrs. Baikie gets them from the Wise Woman."

Isobel, who had been so carefully preparing to be a man, had forgotten all about the fact that her body might betray her. For a moment she was panic-stricken—what else had she forgotten?—and then she smiled and turned away.

From Orphir, Kirkwall was in the opposite direction to Stromness. She would have to pass back through the parish, and her journey of fifteen miles would take hours.

All through the summer night she walked towards Stromness and the ship. On the hills huge bonfires made of gorse peats, like the nests of giant birds, waited for the celebrations tomorrow eve. She had never been so far away from home before, and with each step she felt more and more free. John Scarth had mentioned that the agent was frantic because he hadn't filled the quota of men required and Captain Hanwell was impatient to sail. She was confident they would hire her on the spot. And she wouldn't let them down. Hard work and a full belly, she thought to herself. And trees. He had talked of trees, of forests, of forts made of wood, so much wood around they could never use it up in a million years. The men spent days chopping wood against the long, cold winter. She could do that; she could learn to chop trees as well as any man.

She stopped at the end of the town, sat on a stone wall and ate some bannock and butter from a parcel Jannet had made up for her. Gulls swooped down, hoping for crumbs, but she had eaten everything and licked her fingers. It was a beautiful morning; the sun winking off the bay resembled shoal after shoal of little fishes. Already plumes of smoke were rising from the stone houses; she could smell peat burning and hear the clatter of housewives preparing the morning meal. The agent's house and the harbour of Hamnavoe were just minutes away, at the end of the long and narrow street.

She sat there for a few minutes longer as Isobel Gunn. When she stood up she was John Fubbister, of St. Andrews parish in the Orkney Isles, twenty years of age, labourer for hire. He headed towards the pier, whistling.

WOULD SHE HAVE GOT away with it if Mr. Geddes had not been occupied with the last sentences of his letter to the governor of York Factory and the worry about the overdue bill from his Liverpool tailor? The ship was to sail on the tide and the harbour was full of men shouting and men heaving bundles and barrels and sea-chests into the jolly boat and rowing like mad out to the *Prince of Wales*. There were a few women among the crowd, mothers or sweethearts or sisters of men leaving or men still out there in a land the women could only imagine from the tales of the old-timers or from the yearly letters of their husbands, sons, brothers, lovers—

if their men could write. Small boys were there as well, and
old men and the seabirds crying. Because of privateers and
the war with the French, the ships travelled in convoys, one
destined this time for the top of the Bay, Fort Churchill, the
other, the *Prince of Wales*, for the bottom.

If it sometimes seemed that the Company of Adventurers
took away our youngest and strongest men, as many
claimed, it gave back goodly sums to our merchants—for
Stromness was the last stop before North America. Butcher
meat, water, meal, salt fish were taken on as well as men.
And while the alehouses welcomed the crew, the society of
Stromness and Kirkwall welcomed the captains and officers
with suppers and balls. There was always a great rush on rib-
bons and new frocks from Mr. Leask's Drygoods Store.

As it turned out, it was Mr. Geddes's clerk who dealt
with John Fubbister—he was the last to sign on—read him
out the conditions of service, had him make his mark and
look lively. Six pounds a year, all found. Isobel kept her tam
pulled low as she moved through the crowd and towards a
boat that was just returning to the pier. She jumped in with
half a dozen others, and was rowed away.

No sooner were they up the ladder than the captain gave
the order to raise the anchor. Isobel leaned over the rail, her
back to all the frantic activity of the sailors, and watched the
crowd grow smaller and smaller as they moved out from
the harbour and along under the steep cliffs of Hoy. And
then the open ocean. She'd done it! She'd escaped. She
decided to look out a hammock and a space to call her own.
She didn't mind appearing ignorant—the more ignorant the

better—but once again she kept her head slightly bowed. It was still possible they'd find her out and throw her overboard, or even (would they? could they?) turn back. Soon she could relax a little, but not today. Orders were still being shouted, more sail was unfurled. The ship began to roll from side to side with an easy motion. She started to go below, following two others who were being guided by an "old hand," when the ship gave a sudden, deeper roll and she nearly collided with a man coming up. He cursed softly and was about to pass by when he turned and looked at her. Looked puzzled for a moment, then astonished.

"You!" he cried.

"Shut yer mouth," she said, low and furious. "Shut yer mouth or I'll—"

He showed his white teeth; he laughed at her. "You'll what?"

"I'll say you put me up to hid, then whar will ye be?"

"They won't believe you."

"Oh, they'll believe me, puir innocent lass." And she began to laugh now, as she saw how this seeming disaster could work to her advantage. "A puir farm lass, ignorant, told to do this for a lark. Oh, aye, nivver doubt I can make them believe me. You'll help me with this, like hid or no. You can be my protector—an *old hand* like you. Otherwise—"

"No man would look twice at you."

"That's what I'm countin' on, but don't you count on hid—that captain will believe me."

He nodded, and cursed her.

"That's enough of that," she said. "My name is John

Fubbister, of St. Andrews parish. You know my brother, George. Now, buddo, show me where to put my hammock. Next to yours might be best."

They went below.

SHE LAUGHED WHEN SHE told me this.

"Oh, the look on his face! I think he would have thrown me to the fishes if he could."

"And he kept his word?"

"Aye. What else could he do?" She paused. "But I paid dearly for hid, as you know."

I nodded. "It was a mad undertaking to begin with."

"Hid was that. Hid could end only in tears."

I ARRIVED AT ALBANY FORT in late August 1808, two years after Isobel Gunn.

"Don't you think it's *amusing*," said the chief factor, Mr. Morton, with what seemed to me a false, forced grin, "that we are stuck out here in this moral desert—and that's where we are, my friend, make no mistake—because of a rodent?"

The ship had departed, loaded with a year's inventory of Made Beaver, a few old hands whose contracts had expired, the packet of official letters for the London Committee, plus letters home. I had added my own, to my father and the doctor, at the very last minute. It was a sort of journal of the

major events in my life since I had waved them goodbye at
Hamnavoe. I asked them to read it and then keep it for me,
as I wanted to share my adventure with them and yet have a
record for myself.

Mr. Morton, like God, seemed to have been everywhere
and nowhere in the past several days, but now that salutes
had been fired and the last strains of "Homeward Bound" had
faded from our ears, he had invited me to join him in his
apartment after dinner. He asked me what I knew about the
beaver.

"Very little, I'm afraid."

He then proceeded to enlighten me.

What I was to find amusing, over the months, was his
obsession with this animal; he was busy compiling a kind of
Castorologia, and he showed me some excellent studies, done
in charcoal, that he intended to include. He informed me
that beavers mated for life, that they were supremely intelligent creatures, that they used their flat tails as drums to warn
others of their species of danger, that the tails themselves
were excellent eating, as I would discover before too long.
He had already explained to me the difference between *castor
gras* and *castor sec.* I had not understood (why would I, my
acquaintance with beaver hats so minimal?) that the "greasy
beaver" was prized because, having been well-used by
Natives, the guard hairs had worn off and the fur underneath, the "wool," made soft by wearing, was what was most
in demand by the Worshipful Company of Feltmakers. It
amused him hugely that the fashionable men and women of
Belgravia were unaware that their elegant hats started out as

winter coverings for savages. "How do they get the stink out, I wonder?" He mentioned the castoreum, a waxy substance with a most peculiar odour that is found in the perineal sacs of both sexes. (At this point, he showed me a drawing of something that looked like dried pears.)

"It is reputed to be useful as an anti-spasmodic," he said, "and also as an aphrodisiac. The Company sells it to the perfumers of France."

As he talked, taking sips of a fine old cognac in between revelations about the beaver, I had a chance to study him. My first impression, which I was to modify later on, was of a vain and silly man in his early forties, a man who would be more at home in a parlour than behind a palisade. I had seen already that he was not much liked by the men, but they certainly hopped to do his bidding. He was probably no taller than the Little Emperor, and his features were somehow undeveloped, as though they had been licked again and again by a cow or a cat. His voice, when relaxed, was a kind of drawling sneer, the voice of the educated Englishman. When giving orders, however, he could bark with the best of them.

"Drink up, drink up, man," he said, pushing the bottle in my direction. "There's plenty more. This is the start of our year. Furs out, provisions in. No need to economize yet." Then, keeping his hand on the journals containing his notes and observations on the beaver, he gave me a chilly smile.

"And what of you, Mr. Inkster? Have you mated for life? I assume not, or you wouldn't be here. Although that doesn't stop some," he muttered. "That doesn't stop some. There are

men, your countrymen, sir, and mine, who left wives and
children weeping and waving their handkerchiefs at
Gravesend or the Point of Ness and yet have wives and children here. Country wives, we call 'em—marriage 'according to the custom of the country.' It smacks of the barnyard
to me; does it not smack of the barnyard to you, Mr.
Inkster?"

"The men must get very lonely," I murmured.

"Oh, yes, these are lonely places, and men are men.
Better the natural sin than the unnatural, eh? But the
Company is very worried, Mr. Inkster, very worried indeed.
There is now such a throng of country wives and country
brats at each post, there will soon be more of them than us.
We cannot provide for all this copper-coloured consolation,
Mr. Inkster. Something will have to be done soon. It is a
question not just of morality but of economics. I hope you
will not add to our burden."

He stood up, smiled his thin smile. We said our good-
nights and I went to my bed.

I had asked him about Isobel Gunn. I had not yet seen
her, although I knew of her presence at the fort. Of the
twenty men at Albany, twelve of them were Orkneymen and
eight of these from Mainland. I had hardly stepped from the
sloop to the shore before I was asked if I knew her. I replied
that I knew *of* her, for who in Orkney did not?

"Aye," said one old-timer, the tailor, as I was to discover
later. "Her'll no doot go doon in t' history books, that one."
He said it with a kind of admiration.

"Does she live here at the fort?" I asked.

"Outside," said the man with a chuckle. "Her lives in a tipi; like the Indians. Her and her bairn an' a woman called Mary. The gov'nor made her a cabbin, but her prefers to live outside. Him doesna like her—but him likes the wee boy."

"I should have sent her back a year ago," said the chief factor that night. "I should have sent her back just now—can't think why I didn't."

"Your kind heart, sir," said the surgeon, and winked at me and the two traders who made up our mess. They looked so much alike they could have dropped out of the same egg. I was having trouble remembering which was MacNeil and which was McTavish. The surgeon, a gross young Irishman with an inflamed nose and a gouty leg, was called Mr. Rooney.

"Yes," said Mr. Morton, "I suppose that's it."

"It's not hard to think why she wants to stay here. What would await her at home?"

"Indeed so. I should imagine a disgraced woman is a disgraced woman even in Ultima Thule. Here she has a certain status among our meadow gentry. And the Canadians. And the men. Last year, when they discovered she wished to stay, they sent a delegation to see me. Threatened to quit in a bloc! I was sorely tempted to discharge them all on the spot, but that would have caused even more talk and some of those men were old hands. I needed them and they knew it."

"She hoodwinked them, Mr. Inkster. Hoodwinked us all."

"Do you think the men knew?"

"Swore up and down they didn't."

"One knew at any rate," said McTavish or MacNeil.

"We were not so gullible, perhaps, as we might seem to you or to the Company. The Committee has no idea of the layers of clothing worn at the Bay, layers and layers. In winter to keep from freezing, in summer to keep from being driven mad by the mosquitoes. Women who stay at home, back in the civilized world, in their fashionable gowns, languishing before the fire or on a chaise longue in the garden—well, one can tell almost immediately if they are with child. One can tell with the servant girl or the peasant woman. But here! And she—he—worked willingly and well. A strong young lad, I thought her—Scarth's protegé. And Scarth had been with the Company for years. Good God! If someone is presented to you as a man, is dressed as a man, works as hard as any man, does nothing whatsoever to make you doubt he is a man, why on earth would you suspect he is a woman in disguise? Especially here."

"Indeed." I nodded at him. Years ago, dressed in boys' clothes, she had fooled me. Because she was dressed that way and doing what boys normally did, I had assumed she was a boy. But that was only at first glance. It still seemed quite incredible that she got away with it for more than a year.

As though he had read my mind, the chief said, "She was away a great deal of the time. She was away when she had the child; I wish she'd stayed away. Let the North West Company deal with her."

The surgeon laughed. "I would have given a guinea to have seen old Henry's face!" Then, to me: "We have never figured how she managed the necessary offices. The ordinary labourers are not shy about such things."

"Oh, Scarth had a hand in that, you can be sure," said one of the traders, and smirked. She had obviously been a dinner-table topic for a long time.

"Are you going to let her stay on indefinitely?"

"No, no. But for the time being. We have her working as washerwoman, which she is no witch at, I can tell you, and she acts as a sort of nursemaid to some of the younger children. Perhaps she can help you in the schoolroom in some way?"

I nodded. "And the man who debauched her? Scarth. Where is he in all this?"

"The man whom she says——"

"Very well. The man whom she says is the father of her child. Has he not been called to account?"

Mr. Morton smiled. "Not by anyone here below. He's dead. A great pity, really. An excellent steersman, and he had a certain standing with the other men."

"A pity for Isobel Gunn as well?"

He shrugged. "A woman like that? I have no pity for her, only for the child. You know, the child—James—has become a great favourite. He lifts our spirits. And Albany Fort has the first white child at the Bay. A dubious distinction in the circumstances, but the men seem proud of the fact. Even if he is a *fils de bast*."

Then he changed the subject, asked me a few questions about the morning's lessons and bid me goodnight.

"The Canadians call her *la picotte*," the surgeon said. "'Tis their name for the smallpox. There is even a chief with that name, a survivor of the last great epidemic in '82." Then he

made his adieus, as did the twins, and I went along to my
apartment, my mind full of Isobel Gunn and my emotions a
mix of terrible pity and a certain admiration. I was not a
risk-taker, but I admired risk-takers. I wondered how long it
would have been, if her body had not betrayed her, before
she was unmasked. From skilled woodsman to washerwoman—what a comedown. Had there been a similar
reduction in pay? I wondered. A labourer got six to eight
pounds a year, all found, a washerwoman (and until now,
they would all have been Indian) one pound. Disgrace or
not, she might be better off back in Orkney.

That night I could not sleep. For one thing, I still felt as
though I were at sea, my body was so used to bracing itself
against the roll of the ship. I could not seem to relax into this
new, steadier world. This was not surprising after all those
weeks at sea. I had noticed earlier that I was having some
difficulty walking on dry land. And I had never lived in a
wooden dwelling before. Houses made of stone do not creak;
it was almost like being back on board the *Prince of Wales*.

But it was mostly my mind that kept me sleepless until
the early hours of the following day. I lay awake and thought
about Isobel Gunn and her child. She must have loved this
man Scarth very much to take such a risk. And to get away
with it for such a long time—amazing! I remembered the
girl whom I had mistaken for a boy, rising triumphant over
the cliff, her sling full of eggs and the angry birds wheeling
and diving around her head. Perhaps she was just the sort of
woman to gamble everything for love.

And now, from valued labourer to washerwoman—and

a child to look after, a fatherless child. I had been reading
Marlowe on board the ship.

O I'le leap up to my God!
Who pulles mee downe?

The chief factor's question about my marital status had
also set me to thinking how—with my mother so long dead,
no brothers and sisters and my father my only close relative;
with no wife or sweetheart waiting anxiously for the return
trip of the *Prince of Wales* and letters from a husband or
lover—that perhaps it was time, past time, to take me a
wife. I was thirty-one years old and most of my life had been
taken up with study. And now here I was in a place where no
wives or sweethearts were allowed. Would I succumb to
what Mr. Morton sneeringly referred to as "a little bit of
brown"? I had seen the Native women who came out with
the Albany sloop, acting as interpreters for Captain Hanwell.
I had seen other women and children at the landing stage.
The young women were comely, even beautiful. Captain
Hanwell had said he thought the Cree women were the most
handsome of all the Native women he had seen.

On the voyage out I had become used to the snoring and
grunts and flatulence of other men. The silence of my own
apartment made me all too aware of how alone I was and
how far away from home. Yet along with that there was a general sense of excitement, of not knowing what the next days,
months, years might bring. And of course I wondered some
more about the notorious Isobel Gunn, and how soon I
would get to see her. What on earth had possessed her to

follow her lover to this harsh land, to disguise herself as a man and work among men as one of them?

("A man would, *of course*, think a woman could do such a thing only for love," Isobel said later. "Let them say what they like, I know the truth of hid." She lay her cheek against the child's bright head. "And now you know the truth of hid as well.")

There was another thing that kept me awake. I hadn't asked the question. "How did Scarth die?"

ALBANY FORT WAS A LOG building two storeys high, with a flanker at each corner. Around all this was a palisade and farther out, around the grounds themselves, was a stockade with a single stout gate at front and back. For the first few days I simply marvelled at the size of such a wooden edifice. Even the size of the logs amazed me.

"Are you not afraid of fire?" I asked Mr. Morton.

"Always. That is why pipe smoking is prohibited except at stated times in stated places, and no smoking is allowed in the cabbins. Any man caught is severely punished. Candles, too. I worry excessively about candles. Some of these men, sir, are not moderate in their consumption of beer and English brandy. When they stagger off to bed with their candlesticks, I shudder. That is why the watch checks each cabbin after lights out—to ensure that the lights are truly out. There have been dreadful fires at the posts, but none in my time, thank heaven."

A schoolroom had been set up for me in one of the flankers. Just a few wooden forms for the children to sit on and a tall lectern that I could also use for Divine Service, as Mr. Morton had made it clear that he was happily relinquishing this duty to me. There were some slates and the books that had been donated by the Scottish Society for the Propagation of Christian Knowledge: Bibles, catechisms, Scott's *Good Effects of Prayer*, Watt's *Hymns*, a *Sacred History* by a Mrs. Trimmie, a pronouncing dictionary.

Other than these, I was on my own. I had never taught young children in my life—a far cry from Latin, Greek and the elevated subjects I had served up to the spoiled sons of Lord Pitmillie. This should be easier, except I had been warned that the children were a "mixed bag" (Mr. Morton thought this phrase exceedingly funny and repeated it), and from what I could gather they ranged from the bright sons and daughter of the chief trader to "a couple of savages who are as innocent of their letters as the birds and beasts of the forest." The Company had stipulated that the Native children were to be encouraged in their schooling, but only if they agreed to accept a Christian name. I was more than a little nervous as I stood there on that first morning awaiting them.

They all came at once, in a ragged crocodile. At the rear, hurrying them along, was Isobel Gunn, and strapped to her back in a carrying cradle was her wee boy.

THE HONOURABLE GENTLEMEN in London were primarily interested in the number and quality of the furs sent back each year in the Company ships, and although that was the whole reason for the factories at the Bay, we had another duty: to stay warm, well-fed and healthy. Out there we were more or less responsible for our own survival. The Company's servants chopped the wood that made the fires that cooked our food (most of it shot or trapped or hooked) set forth upon the table. When I think back now on the amount of fish, flesh and fowl we managed to kill, of the number of beaver and marten, rabbit and lynx trapped, it is a wonder there are any living creatures, except man and the insects, still alive in Rupert's Land. Mr. Morton, who wrote a fine hand, kept a daily journal of all our activities, mentioning also the wind and weather, the comings and goings of groups of Indians, the arrival and departure of those sent off with inland cargo. Each day each man at Albany Fort had to be accounted for, to prove that he was earning his keep. The evening of the day on which I started teaching, Mr. Morton showed me the journal. There were not many entries as yet, for the books ran from late August to late August and were sent home with the ship.

"This day Mr. Inkster began with his pupils in the new schoolroom." I was mentioned at the end of a list that showed the armourer busy making locks and hinges, the tailor cutting out new trade coats that would be given as presents to the "captains" of the various groups of Indians when they brought in the furs in the spring. These "captain's outfits" were a parody of a military uniform and very much prized by the wearer.

The carpenter was making sleds; some men were brewing beer, others grinding oatmeal. Even the sick were busy cleaning the house and yard or picking oakum.

"Nothing philosophical, you understand, Mr. Inkster, just the facts of our daily life. No musings on the role of Providence in casting us up in this dreadful place; no discussion of the habits, good or bad, of our country gentry. I have another, private, book for that."

Each day, before dinner, he wrote in the official journal, then closed the book and locked it in a drawer.

"It becomes tedious, you know," he said, "after the first year. The occupations of the men depend upon the seasons—when the river freezes over, when the ice breaks up. Out to the goose tents in autumn and spring, out with the fishnets when the water runs free, off to the traplines in winter. Busy busy busy: we are a regular hive of activity here. And I am the recording angel of it all."

"Do the governors read every page of the journal—once it gets back to London?"

"I doubt it, but that doesn't mean I can skip or prevaricate. It is part of my contract, this journal. And you are to keep a record as well, Mr. Inkster. It need not be daily, but the Company wants to know how you get on, wants to see if their little experiment is worthwhile."

"I hope to make it so, sir."

"Hmmm. There is something in the Bible—is there not?—about silk purses and sow's ears?" He handed me a large ledger in which I was to record attendance and the progress of each of my pupils. No doubt it is still in the

Company's offices somewhere, along with the others. Isobel's name is in there, of course, but like Mr. Morton, I recorded nothing but the facts. My private thoughts and worries I learned to keep locked away, not in a drawer but in my heart.

THE MEETING WITH JOHN SCARTH, which should have been her undoing, was, in the end, quite literally a blessing in disguise. Her hammock was slung above his when they slept, and when the necessities of Nature called her, they called him as well. He treated the whole thing as a private joke and went around with such a great grin on his face, showing his small white teeth, that some of the old hands took to teasing him or whistling "The Handsome Cabin Boy." Except of course she wasn't, with her damaged face.

In a quiet moment, returning from the galleries, she said, "Do you have a wife—out there?"

He smiled. "What do you think? Most of the men have Indian wives or sweethearts. 'Twould be unnatural otherwise."

A new cause for worry. Would the Indian women spy her out?

"They live outside the forts," he said. "Except for the officers' wives. They serve us well."

"They serve—?"

"The lad blushes," he said. "Oh, yes, they serve us in that way, of course, but in other ways. They know things—how

to make us moccasins, how to dress meat and prepare pem-
mican, how to lead us through forests and rivers."

The next day was mending day on the ship, and as Isobel
stood watching the sailors spread out on the deck, sewing on
patches, replacing buttons, Scarth passed by and made a rude
gesture in the direction of the men. He spit.

"And we don't do any of that," he said to her. "The country women mend our clothes."

The temperature was dropping; she shivered in her
smock.

"Come," he said, "I'll find you a gansey—we can't have
you falling sick. Once we're at the Bay you'll get your outfit,
but for now I'd best help you out."

She followed him down into their dark, close-smelling
quarters. In his sea-chest he found a heavy gansey. She put it
on and went back up on deck. The vastness of the ocean
exhilarated her. They'd lost sight of their sister ship four days
earlier and since then there had been, once or twice, sails in
the far distance. Nothing now. She felt detached from everything she'd ever known, doubly detached, as she was not
part of the ship's crew. She was fascinated by the running of
the ship, how quickly the men responded to orders,
although she was somewhat afraid of the sails, those yards
and yards of canvas and rope turning this way and that,
enticing the wind, one moment big-bellied and the next
flapping listlessly like clothes on a line. Sometimes, she told
me, she felt as though she were on the back of some enormous bird, letting herself be carried to her destination. She
was afraid of John Scarth, but she didn't think he'd make any

trouble, not now, and once she got to the Bay . . . well, she knew how strong she was, strong as an ox, strong as the next young man. She looked down at her hard, callused hands and feet with pleasure. She'd earn her wages and maybe in five years she'd come back, give George the money to buy a piece of land for them all. Or maybe not. Set herself up with a shop—only she'd have to learn to read and do sums. She smiled at her fancies.

One thing she knew for sure: she would never be a wife. There was a surplus of women in Orkney, swarms of spinsters who lived with their parents or brothers and sisters, helping with the children, sitting in the coldest corners, turning into old gossips. The young ones made up rhymes about them. Some suffered worse fates, became beggars, went from door to door with their caisies on their backs, requesting a measure of meal. With the wind in her face and her adventure just begun, she made a vow to heaven that she would never be one of those old grannies, never.

The first mate saw John Fubbister standing idle and put him to work holystoning the deck.

Two years later, when I sailed on the same ship to the same destination, contracted to the Company of Adventurers as schoolmaster for the sum of thirty-two pounds a year, all found, I stared at the empty sea with a feeling of heavy dread, as though I had just made a supper of stones. I, who loved books and the companionship of other thinking, questioning, intelligent men—what had I been thinking of when I lied my way through Mr. Skaill's questions concerning my aptitudes and beliefs? My cabin mates—two returning traders and the other teacher, who was destined for Moose Factory—were hardly interested in a lively exchange of ideas, the first two because their lives were dedicated to the adding up of animal skins, the third because he was so full of the Word of God he had no words of his own. In my sea-chest I carried Francis Bacon, the sermons of Jonathan Edwards, the complete plays of William Shakespeare, Dante's "Letter to Con Grande," as well as my Bible and certain other religious tomes. With whom would I talk? Who would help me wrestle with the terrible problems of free will and predestination? And what made me think I would find any answers at the Bay? My father and the doctor had both thought it was an excellent idea. There was no living vacant at the moment, and I had made it clear I did not want to return to the awkward and humiliating position of being tutor to a family who would look down their noses at me.

"Ach!" cried the doctor. "If I were young again and free, I would not hesitate."

The doctor's wife had died the year before, but his daughter, Helen, was married to the headmaster at Kirkwall Grammar School. There were grandchildren as well. Ties of memory and blood bound him to the place. He and my father went weekly to their wives' graves.

I wanted to tell these two good men what a hypocrite I was, but I looked at their kind, eager faces and kept silent.

"You are a pair of old romantics," I said to my father that night.

"Perhaps so. But what a wonderful opportunity to serve God and have an adventure at the same time."

"I shall miss you, Father. And a letter will come but once a year."

"I shall miss you as well. The doctor and I shall spend many an evening talking of you and our prayers shall be with you always."

That Sunday his sermon was on the parable of the five talents and at the end of it he announced to the congregation that his namesake and only son would be leaving shortly to act as schoolmaster to a group of children at the bottom of Hudson Bay. The men all came up to shake my hand and the women whispered how proud my blessed mother would have been.

The night before the ship sailed, my father gave me his pocket watch and a new chain.

"Father, I cannot take this."

"No, no, you must. The doctor has two, from both his father and his mother's father, so he intends to give one to me."

"This is not right. That watch is as much a part of you as your pipe. More so."

"You will need a watch; a teacher needs a timepiece."

"I will cherish it."

"Good." He gave it an extra polish with his handkerchief and handed it over. "Do you still have the lock of your mother's hair?"

"Aye. Pressed between a fold of paper and tucked in my Bible."

"Good. That is the one thing I have taken from the watch—from the back. Perhaps now you will replace mine with yours?"

I nodded, unable to speak, and as I stood on the deck of the *Prince of Wales* I remembered a winter afternoon, years before, when the doctor had stopped off on his way back from a visit to the poor.

"Ach, Magnus," he said, warming himself in front of the fire, "you have the easier calling, you know."

"Because the soul is easier to care for than the body? Don't you believe it!"

"Not quite. Because the soul does not stink. God knows I pity the poor, and I do what I can to relieve their pain—pay for the cordials myself, slip a coin to a neighbour so she'll keep an eye on an old, sick, solitary dame—but the stench in some of these places! It is the stench that nearly defeats me."

"I visit those cottages too," said my father quietly, "and so does Morag. That is the stench of sickness and of poverty."

"I know, I know. I'm speaking metaphorically, and perhaps, to God the Father, some souls stink to high heaven. But I wish there were more soap and water and less drink among the poor of this parish. I have just come from a dirty old woman who fell down while drunk and broke her hip. A drunken old woman is an abomination—truly."

"Why more so than a drunken old man?" said my mother, sliding her darning egg under another one of my holey stockings, shaking her head and smiling at me as she did so. I was home for the winter holidays.

"Why . . . why . . ." the doctor struggled to reply. "Why because women are made of finer clay than men. It distresses me to see a woman sunk so low."

"Your distress is mixed with disgust?"

"Yes," he said slowly, "I am sorry to say it is."

"I thought," said my mother, putting the stocking aside and rising to get the tea (she often did this as a way of leaving a conversation while technically having the last word), "I thought that we were made from Adam's rib. Have you heard otherwise?"

"She's got you, William," said my father, laughing. "Your nice distinction won't hold."

I remember that afternoon particularly, not because of what was said, but because of the sewing basket on the low table near my mother, the darning wool and the cotton and silks and the small scissors she used to trim her handiwork. That basket was never far from her side. If I closed my eyes, I could see her dark curls bent over the stocking and then her merry face lifted to tease the doctor about his prejudices. I can smell the peat fire mixed with the horsey smell of the doctor, and feel the chill air when I ran from the warmth of the parlour to the outside to fix the oatbag on the doctor's horse.

And if I closed my eyes I could see a later scene, not so very much later, with my mother laid out in her flower-sprigged dress, her dear face as calm and removed as a statue, and remember how, in the few moments just before she was to be carried to the cemetery, my father asked if he and I could be alone with her. He went to her sewing basket and, taking out the wee scissors, cut off two locks of her beautiful hair, one for each of us. And how we then held each other and wept uncontrollably, as though we were two who had been tipped roughly out of a boat we had thought was safe and were now on our way to drowning.

For several days the temperature had been dropping, and as we entered Hudson Strait, a little more than four weeks into our journey, I shivered even in my thick gansey and sheepskin jacket, a gift from my patron, James Skaill. The sailors worked so hard that they seemed to be in a constant sweat and even the men taken on as servants for the Bay were now busily engaged in menial tasks, yet I had little to do but stare out at the vast expanse of water or perambulate with Mr. Marwick, the schoolmaster bound for Moose Factory. Mr. Marwick walked always with a Bible in his hand, and knowing a little of the Papish rituals (as schoolboys we exchanged such information as we had), I nicknamed him Extreme Unction. He bored me silly, but at least he took exercise, unlike the traders, who spent their time smoking and playing cards. One morning, as I was standing by the rail, feeling as though my bones had turned to glass, Captain Hanwell invited me to step down to his cabin at any time, even if he were not present, as a fire was always lit therein.

This was a godsend, and I took full advantage of his kind offer, alternating my frozen state on deck with my thawed state in the captain's cabin. For we had now entered such a strange and mysterious world, a world of such beauty and terror, that I could not bear to miss it for the sake of a few frozen fingers and toes.

Although I doubt there was a soul in Orkney who hadn't heard of Hudson Bay or the Company that bore its name, few actually knew what it looked like or where the forts were in relation to one another. The Company was careful with its maps and even letters home were censored to ensure that those not involved in the business remained hazy on such subjects. It wasn't until I myself was aboard ship and the recipient of extra hospitality from Captain Hanwell that I actually saw a map and saw exactly where I was going.

"It's a big place, Rupert's Land," he said, "and the Bay itself is vast. You are headed down here, to the bottom of the Bay, to Albany Fort. Looks like an udder with a single teat, don't it?" he said, as he traced the route of the *Prince of Wales* with his finger. "And we don't actually land at the fort—the water in the river is too shoal. We dock in the roadstead outside and offload from there. It's fifteen miles from where we dock to where you'll be ending up."

"Do you know the chief factor, Mr. Morton?"

Captain Hanwell laughed. "I wouldn't say as I *know* him, but I'm acquainted with him. He's fairly new at this game and a bit—well—a bit stand-offish. Didn't come up through the ranks like most of 'em. English."

I laughed. "But you're English."

"I'm a Londoner, man!" As if that settled the matter.

I stood staring down at the map. So many forts, little dots or X's, locating but not revealing anything about the life within. The captain seemed to sense my mood.

"A strange life that. I'd hate it m'self."

"Some might think your life equally as strange."

"Aye, they might. There's a French saying about that, but I don't remember it. I love the sea, but I have the best of all worlds. Regular voyages—which demand no small amount of navigation skills—and time at home with my wife and family, who are always pleased to see me. Then, just as the

novelty wears off, I'm away again. The Company pays me
year round, on sea or land. I'm just as much a 'loyal servant'
as the officers of the forts or the men who work in them.
I grew up poor, Mr. Inkster; security is a grand thing."

With that, he knocked out his pipe, nodded and left me
still looking at the map. The Albany River, the Moose River,
the Churchill River—far inland, more lakes and rivers. The
original forts had all been built right on the edge of the Bay,
but now there were inland posts as well. I wondered if I
would get a chance to travel, imagined myself in a birchbark
canoe or trekking on snowshoes with congenial companions.

As it turned out, I never left the post at Albany Fort. It
was Isobel, as John Fubbister, who got to see more of the
Company's vast trading empire.

"I was born for hid," she told me. "To me, it was the best
life in the whole wide world."

Except for the fear that was always there at the back of
the mind—the fear she would be found out.

The captain was needed on deck, but later he said to me:
"You are from Orphir, Mr. Inkster?"

"Aye."

"Are you acquainted with Isobel Gunn?"

"I am acquainted with her story, or at least the bits of
gossip that have come back to us."

"Poor wench. She is at Albany Fort, you know. You will
see her soon enough. They don't know what to do with her."

I hadn't known. I wanted to quiz the captain on the subject of Isobel Gunn, but he said no more.

We had been several days in rain and thick fog, the ship

slowed down to what would have been a crawl, were she a crawling creature. The shouts of the lookout and the commands of the captain and first mate came muffled to our ears, as though we heard through layers and layers of wet wool. We knew there was ice all around us, and the shouts of the men indicated that we were in no little danger, but we couldn't really see the ice, only feel its chill breath and sometimes discern huge masses of dark somethings; they could have been mountains or monsters.

Then, on the evening of the fourth day, the air cleared just before sunset and we were presented with such a glittering world (I could not help thinking of Bunyan's "world of wonders") that I gasped as though I had been plunged, suddenly, into another dimension altogether. The water took on a golden tint and the clouds above were now a dusky red, now a deep, deep blue. And all around us were the fantastic forms of icebergs. I saw palaces and barns and enormous creatures, reminding me of my father's stories of Ymir, the Frost Giant and the world of ice. It was as though I were inside the very mind of God, or a god, for there was a terror about all this that chilled my very heart. One of the bergs roared like thunder from a crack through which the sea was bursting. Towns of ice, statues of ice, cliffs of ice, pavements made of ice as white as alabaster. During the days we spent in Hudson Strait, I never quite lost my feeling of dread and yet this new world also excited me, there was such beauty in it.

In the daytime we could see seals basking on the ice and once a bear, nearly the colour of ice himself, quietly padding towards his dinner.

In the night sky the aurora borealis put on such displays of light that the eye and brain grew dizzy at the sight of them. Streamers of light shooting upwards, zig-zagging across the sky, fading out and then beginning again. The captain told me that the Eskimos believe the northern lights are the souls of their people playing football and making merry, not unlike our own tradition of the Merry Dancers.

If I closed my eyes and ignored the cold, I could almost imagine, from the roaring and crackling and general noise of the icebergs, that we were being pursued by a giant fire. I thought of Niflheim and Muspell, the two regions on either side of the Great Void, one frozen, the other burning. Were the myths of the old Norsemen inspired by places like this? And does not that old world end with a holocaust? Mr. Marwick, the other schoolmaster, told me at dinner that he was quite overcome with God's grandeur; for once I could agree with him.

SOMETIME IN THE COURSE of that first winter, Isobel saw the Berdash, whom she called, as we do in Orkney, the Him-Har, although he was not a true hermaphrodite but only a man who wished to be a woman. He was one of the sons of a famous chief, and his father despaired of him. He was distantly related, by blood or obligation, to one of the Home Guard, a woman called Mary. Apparently there are creatures of this sort among many, if not all, of the Indian tribes. He was dressed as a woman, walked and sat as a woman,

and occasionally carried on his back, in a little cradle, a
wooden baby.

The men teased him and made crude jokes, plied him
with liquor, which made him act even more outrageously; he
began to brag about all the "husbands" he had had, offering
himself up to the assembly. He flirted and pouted until one
of the officers said it was enough and he was flung outside.
Isobel, who stayed on the edge of the group, saw John Scarth
turn and look directly at her, giving his little smile. The
Berdash came several times to the fort and was always a
source of great amusement. Isobel stayed out of his way; she
had a feeling he would recognize her as a woman immediately and was afraid John Scarth might set something up to
test him.

The strange thing was, the men said, he was very brave,
an excellent shot and could outrun any man when he chose
to do so.

To the bored men he was a diversion, and obviously, in
some instances, more than that. In the two years I was at the
Bay I saw him only once, but because he was part of Isobel's
story, I often wondered about him and those like him. In
Orkney we used the term chiefly to describe animals who
are born with double sets of genitalia, although I once heard
the doctor discussing, with my father, a child he had been
attending. But I knew of no man, with a man's parts, who
behaved like a woman, dressed like a woman in petticoats
and shawls, and offered himself to be used as a woman. My
beloved Shakespeare was full of mistaken identity—always
girls dressed as boys—and that just added to the fun of the

piece. There was romantic love involved, but never this kind of Mistress Quickly bawdiness. For what the Berdash presented himself as was a whore, and that was deeply disturbing. The world of Rupert's Land and the world of the Company posts was a world in which the traditional values of manliness held sway. In such a world the Berdash was completely out of place. Except for one thing.

Mr. Morton wondered why the chief, his father, did not have him killed.

OVER THE WEEKS, AS SHE progressed from her letters to the actual writing of words—she never learned to spell properly, but I let that pass for the time being—she related her history, from the time she left the farm until the morning I saw her ushering the children into the schoolroom. She had told no one, except the Cree woman Mary, what had happened. Scarth was dead, but even if he had been alive, his version of events would have differed sharply from hers. The men all assumed that Scarth had been her lover, and the Berdash, who knew the truth, kept quiet.

"Why did you not go to Mr. Morton and explain before Scarth died? Call upon the Berdash to recount what he saw?"

"The Berdash comes and goes. He was no here when I returned with James. And our chief thinks he is disgusting. Would he put any faith in the words of such a thing?"

"No," I said. "You are probably right. And with the culprit dead, what was the point?"

"I think Mr. Alexander Henry might have believed me, but at that time John Scarth was still alive. I was afraid of him; he had said he would kill me if I told."

"But he wasn't there—at Pembinah."

"No, but his friends were. Hid could have been arranged. Things like that can be arranged. I just let hid be. And there was the child to worry about—my son."

Much later, when I came to look back on her story, I was surprised at how intimate she became—in some of the details. Did she think that because I had been trained for the church she was making some sort of confession? I was terribly moved by her absolute trust in me at the same time as I was amazed at the education she was giving me, an alphabet of a woman's anatomy, if you will.

Her breasts, for instance. When she said "breasts" to me in her soft island accent, I was shocked. This was not a word a young woman used when talking to a young man. Her head was bent and so she did not notice my discomfort.

She had considered herself a man for so long, it puzzled her when her breasts became tender and began to swell. It was almost as though when she put on a man's clothes and a man's name, she assumed she had put on a man's body as well. She had been John Fubbister for eleven months, nearly a year, and so at first she did not connect what had happened in March to the changes occurring to her body. Her nausea she put down to overeating, for "John" was always being teased about his appetite; her fatigue, a certain heaviness of limb and a desire to sleep, to the need for a spring tonic. It had been a long, hard winter and she had been out at the goose tents for a month when she noticed the first changes. The men had gorged themselves on fresh meat and several others had complained of stomach aches or weariness. How well they ate would depend on the success of the goose hunt. Hundreds of birds were killed in a single day, thousands in a month. They were plucked and cleaned by the Native women, who gathered the feathers in sacks, to be weighed and sold at a later date. Often the air was so full of feathers it seemed as though the blizzards of winter had returned.

John Fubbister had become an excellent shot and enjoyed the outdoor life. Why, then, this nausea, this reluctance to pull himself up out of sleep? By the middle of June, she knew she was with child.

Her anger was directed both at Scarth (who was no longer at Albany, but as soon as the river broke up had been transferred to Eastmain, where one of their crack steersmen had died of putrid sore throat) and at her own body, which had trapped her and could give away her true identity. Although Scarth was her first carnal experience, she had been listening to women talk about their bodies from the time she was a babe; she knew there were ways to get rid of unwanted pregnancies—certain herbs and nostrums. If she had been at home, she could have gone to Jannet or the Wise Woman, but she was not at home. The women of the Home Guard would know, but she knew few words of their language, and would they keep her secret? Some of them were washerwomen for the men, some were country wives. It was too dangerous to reveal herself to them.

She bound her breasts and ribs with bands of flannel,

saying she had strained a muscle and was more comfortable so; then, once back at the fort, she threw herself into a frenzy of activity, hewing, hauling, running when she could have walked. When the roof of the main house needed repairing, she was the first up the ladder. And she, who had been abstemious, even indulged in quantities of "English brandy," hoping the gin would bring the baby on.

"Men got the bloody flux from time to time," she said to me calmly. "I could have explained hid away."

Nothing worked. The spirits made her dizzy and sick, and all she got for her physical efforts that summer was praise from the chief factor and remarks from the surgeon (she had lined up with the rest of the men and endured her spoonfuls of sulphurated molasses) that it would appear his remedies worked some of the time on some of the men. She even prayed, in an incoherent, jumbled way. Prayed for God to take the baby.

What did she imagine would happen to her, I asked, if she were discovered?

"Driven awa'," she replied. "Cast out."

I have tried many times to imagine a similar situation for a man, some sort of analogy to what she was going through at that time. The fear of being "found out" or unmasked, shown to be other than what you have pretended, yes, of course. All of us fear in our hearts at some time or other that our mean little selves will be revealed. But to have your accuser growing inside you—that I cannot imagine. To be "discovered" by yourself, damned by yourself, and then to face the world, which will damn you double.

I had asked Mr. Morton for extra time with Isobel; I pointed out that it was useful for her to learn to read and write, that when——*if*——she was sent back to Orkney, it might help her to have these basic skills.

"I can't see how," he replied. "For who would engage her? I think perhaps you are simply educating her above her station. She may get ideas. The child, now, the child is another matter. A *tabula rasa*, Mr. Inkster, a *tabula rasa* on which, in spite of his unfortunate beginnings, great things might be written."

I had been looking at some of Mr. Morton's sketches, including an excellent rendition of a beaver's skull. How could such a popinjay have the artist's eye? His drawings continued to amaze me——and to amaze the men. If he were in good humour, he would amuse himself by making quick studies: the tailor bent over his cloth, two trappers on snowshoes, a group of Indians before the window of the store on trading day. The men loading the boats. Even the Native women, of whom he spoke so disparagingly.

"You are a veritable artist, sir."

"Nonsense." But he blushed with pleasure. "It is something to pass the time."

Rather hesitantly, he handed me over some more sketches, mostly of the child, one very strange of Isobel, just the edges of her jacket and her large hands holding the boy, holding him out, as though offering him to the viewer.

Mr. Morton was very proud of his family connections; his mother's brother, a prosperous banker, was on the Committee. It was at his uncle's suggestion that he had applied for

a commission to the Bay. A great deal of money had been
invested and the uncle wanted to have someone on the
"inside" sending him back reports. When I asked about his
name—"Morton is a Scots name, is it not?"—he said, "Yes.
My mother, now a widow, was unfortunate enough to marry
a man from Inverness. My uncle is a Mr. Coville." Now I
asked him if his uncle had ever seen any of his nephew's
drawings.

"Oh, once or twice, when I was a lad. He is a man of
affairs, Mr. Inkster. He has no time for trifles."

"But these are not trifles, Mr. Morton."

He gave me a strange look. "I am dependent upon my
uncle, Mr. Inkster. My mother was widowed young. Without
the munificence of her brother, we should have been
undone."

"But I should think the Company would be happy—
delighted—to have such a record of life at the Bay. I say this
most sincerely. Was not Prince Rupert himself an accomplished artist?"

He merely smiled and shook his head. "Now if I could
make maps!"

I returned him to the subject of lessons for Isobel Gunn.
How she was too busy, during the regular hours, keeping the
children in order and caring for her own child, to benefit
from my instruction then. I was at my most learned and persuasive—how education could lift even the most backward
from the slough of despond, how the great John Calvin himself had advocated basic education for all. I even indulged in
a little sophistry and tried not to be ashamed of it later. If the

Committee felt it important enough to send schoolmasters all the way from Orkney to educate *half-breeds*, would they not want this ignorant white girl to learn to read and write?

He finally agreed—"So long as it does not interfere with her other duties"—and I went away satisfied.

And so, in my official journal I could add the name of Isobel Gunn to the list of scholars and report that by November 5, Saturday, "This week the scholars having regularly attended, perceiving still further amendment. Begun John MacNeil to write small hand, also received to school Will McIntosh, aged about five years, began him in the Alphabets. The woman Isobel Gunn makes progress in same."

TWO THINGS SAVED HER FROM discovery and the first was the climate. As Mr. Morton had pointed out to me, one stays covered up all year round at the Bay. 'Tis only in early spring and perhaps for a month in the autumn that one can go about with sleeves butted up. The snow stayed late that year and the insects began early. Men cursed, their faces swollen almost beyond recognition; each man walked in a nimbus of mosquitoes, and heaps of mosquitoes piled up in front of doors. Their whine and their sting drove the men nearly mad and the animals were frantic. Calomel was so thickly spread on hands and faces that Albany Fort resembled a leper colony. The chief, the surgeon and the other officers never stepped outside without their hats covered in protective veils of

green gauze. The men were nearly mutinous and wanted to
know why there was no gauze available to them. Mr. Morton
said these hats were a new thing and had been sent out only
on trial. He promised the men he would order green veiling
for all with the next ship. The Company must have turned
him down, for there were no veils for any but the officers
when I was there.

The old hands agreed they had never seen such things
before, and mutiny was averted. The mosquitoes were so terrible that men took to wearing more than one pair of
trousers, more than one shirt; the devils could bite right
through their clothing. At night the sounds of slaps and
curses could be heard throughout the men's building. Ears
ran bright with blood and sweat, for the temperature rose to
an unprecedented high in July. Still the duties and chores
went on, day after day. But Isobel was gone by then, sent as
part of a brigade to the Company's post at Pembinah. They
went the long route, past Osnaburgh House and Lac Seul,
then to the Winnipeg River and up the Red. One of the men
died on the way; they pulled in to bury him quickly and set
a small cairn of stones and a wooden cross to mark the spot.
She was unsure what he died of; she said she remembered
little about that inland trip (more than fifteen hundred miles)
and it passed in a kind of dream. During the days, she rowed;
during the nights, she slept. She was withdrawing into herself and the men teased her, saying she missed her chum and
protector, John Scarth. She spent most of her time, even
while her body responded to the demands of the boat and
the river, planning what she was going to do. She had heard

that a Native woman could be on the trail all day, then when her time came would disappear into the woods, catching up to the party a few hours later, the child snug in a moss basket on her back. Would she be able to do that when her time came? She had dim recollections of her mother groaning and crying out; did the women in the forest cry out, or were they able, somehow, to control their pain? She knew there would be pain; childbirth was a subject the farm women never ceased talking about. And they did not give birth alone. If the gripper could not get there, a neighbour took her place and other women sat up with the new mother and child. She had never felt so alone in her life. She willed the boats to go faster so that she would be on dry land soon; her legs suffered terrible cramps in the confined space of the boat and she was glad for any rain showers, for then there was water in the boat and she could safely wet herself. Whenever possible, she managed to keep her trousers as wet as she could. Everyone stank and was lousy by the end of such a journey; she did not stand out from the rest.

On September 12, the two Albany boats arrived at the Company's fort at Pembinah and the men were put to work almost immediately, getting in stores of wood and making the building as snug as possible against the winter. Isobel ate buffalo meat for the first time, and the baby, who had quickened in August—"'Twas as if I had swallowed a bird"—began to kick. She complained of the cold and added another layer to her clothing. One of the men said he was getting a belly on him like a pregnant woman, and although her heart seemed to stop in her chest, they all laughed and no more was made of the remark. She did not like Mr. Heney, the new chief of the post; there was something shifty about him, and the men stayed out of his way. Christmas passed with little in the way of merriment. Heney read the Divine Service, and they were given extra rations of meat and spirits. The world outside the fort was a swirl of snow and fierce winds, and when the men went out they went in twos and threes, never alone. Then, on the twenty-eighth of December, it cleared and Isobel was sent with two others, on snowshoes, down to the North West Company fort to beg of candles, since, with the extra men, their ration would not last. Various presents to Alexander Henry were also sent down and some letters. Although the two companies were rivals, the men at inland posts often helped each other out if supplies ran low.

Twice Isobel fell; she was clumsy and awkward and the others became annoyed with her for slowing them down. She was almost mad with fear and wished she knew how to bring the baby on so that she could step off the trail and into the snow-laden trees, give birth and leave the child there for the wolves to find. She could tell the others she was ill and was turning back.

Mr. Alexander Henry invited the three men to stay for the dance the next night. Isobel could hardly say no, and she wondered if perhaps it wouldn't turn out to be a good thing. In all the noise and merriment she could sneak off, if necessary, and no one would miss her.

"How did it happen?" I asked her.

There was a rigid hierarchy within and without the Company forts: the officers, the men, the Natives.

Three campfires at night if Mr. Morton and any officers were with them, two if they weren't.

In March, long before the ice on the river had begun to break up, Isobel had been sent, along with Scarth and some others, to see what they could shoot or snare to augment the dwindling rations. Some of the Home Guard went with them.

They moved through the white world on snowshoes. Once she had mastered these, she told me, she felt like a bird moving across the surface of the snow. Two men pulled a sledge with provisions, as they had left the dogs behind.

The snow glittered and glistened and the sun was so bright they had to squint. Scarth told how the men at Churchill had learned to make bone eye-masks from the Eskimos; the masks had narrow slits to let them see where they were going, but their eyes were protected from the glare. He was a good story-teller and liked to sit around the fire at night telling stories from his life at the Bay. He had been a Company servant for fifteen years and was considered an authority on most things. Isobel now knew that he had a wife and three children back in Firth and a country wife at Martin's Falls, a woman he had grown tired of. He had lately taken up with one of the Home Guard women, but she was very jealous.

"I'm a bit afraid of her," he said, and smiled his tight little smile.

"What d'ye think she'll do to ye, John?"

"Aye, which part of you will she damage first? She's a witch with a gun, that one. You want to watch yersel'."

On any journey, Scarth kept close by her, as he did inside the fort. The men had long ago accepted that John Fubbister was Scarth's protegé. Something had been promised to the family; some obligation was involved. John was not much for the drink, but Scarth said the father had been like that too, the drink went straight to his head, killed him in the end. The men nodded. Most had known someone like that, and they looked with a certain pity on the lad. Isobel knew that the longer he kept quiet about her, the greater her hold over him. His moment to speak out, when the Company ship had arrived last August, was long gone and he had said nothing. She, on the other hand, could come forward at any time and compromise him forever. Like a drowning man, she could pull him down with her. He was a steersman and was soon to be made chief steersman—or so the rumour went—with an increase in his already substantial wages. He had just as much to lose as she did.

But she liked her life at the Bay. As the months went on and the new year came, she settled more and more easily into her role as John Fubbister; she hardly thought of herself as Isobel Gunn any more. And she did not think about the future, but lived from day to day. When the men talked of home and the money they were laying by against the time when they had fulfilled their contracts, money that might be used to buy a small piece of land, when they dreamed out loud about a wife and children, a few black cattle and the smell of the tangle and the sea, she stayed silent.

"Hiv thee a sweetheart, John? Is there a bonny wee lass dreamin' of your return? A brawly lad like yersel' must have a sweetheart?"

She smiled and shook her head. Perhaps they thought her damaged face made her shy, for they never pushed too hard.

"Aye, wael, yer young yet."

The first day they had trapped only a few hares, but after eating from the communal pot, the pipes came out and, warm in her heavy clothing, drowsy from the food and exercise, she stretched out by the fire, curled into herself the way the dogs did. She liked sleeping out, even on this frigid night. She liked the sense of the vast, star-pebbled sky above, and even the howling of the wolves didn't bother her. One of the Home Guard had said that a stag had come to him in a dream, that soon there would be a big kill and full bellies. One of the men said it was about time; he was so full of salt this and salt that he was afraid he was turning into a pillar of salt, like that lassie in the Bible.

The fire from the Indian camp was not far off. She wondered what they talked about. Were all men alike? She was a little afraid of the Native men, and she avoided the women in case they found her out. (But always a pat on the head or a smile for the kiddies, who seemed to her healthy and happy and loved. The chief ranted on about the half-breeds, but since they were mostly the children of his own officers, there was little he could do. The men said he was probably the only officer at the Bay who didn't have a country wife and half a dozen children. They speculated about this and sometimes made crude jokes.) She curled farther into her capote and blanket-roll and fell asleep to the breathy sounds of a mouth organ in the still air. "Will ye no awa' tae bide awa', will ye no . . ."

At dawn they were awakened by one of the Indians with his finger to his lips. Silently they stood, silently they tied on their snowshoes and picked up their guns. In single file they followed the Indians into the trees until they approached a clearing, where they were motioned to stop. On the other side was a magnificent stag, the rising sun just touching his body and burnishing it so that he seemed a creature made of metal, not of flesh. He appeared to be looking straight at them and yet he didn't move. Scarth nodded and the lead Indian slowly raised his gun. In the second before the shot reached him the stag sensed his danger and made as to turn, but it was too late. He sank to his knees in the snow and a second shot killed him.

Isobel and another man went back for the sledge, then the deer was quickly eviscerated and skinned where he had fallen. After the tongue had been cut out and given to the Indian who had fired the first shot, the head, with its large eyes and magnificent antlers, was carefully wrapped (the surgeon knew how to preserve such things, and it would go on the wall in the officers' mess).

The snow was covered in blood and the innards steamed in the cold air. Once Scarth glanced at Isobel to see how she was enjoying this, challenging her with his little smile as his knife sliced and separated meat from bone.

"Come here, John," he said. "You must have a lesson in butchery."

"Aye," said one of the others. "Each must do his bit. Come, John, and have a go."

She was not squeamish; it was not the blood or the thick metallic smell of it that made her hesitate. She had a hard time explaining it to me. Although she was not one who thought consciously of beauty, and she saw animals primarily as useful (dogs, horses) or as food (bears, deer, fish, geese), this was the first stag she had ever seen. The sight of that splendid animal, with the sun on his red coat, his great presence there in the forest, had moved her in a way she couldn't really explain. She said that she understood why the Indians talked to it, apologized to it even though they needed to kill it and were pleased they had done so. The killing was necessary, and yet some sort of acknowledgement had to be made, the recognition that a fellow creature had been sacrificed to that necessity. These were the feelings that washed over her and made her hang back. Not for long, however. No shirkers were allowed.

They went back and broke camp and headed towards the fort. There would be one more night of sleeping rough, but no one grumbled. With a job well done, the men were in a fine mood and no hurry.

That night there were venison steaks and bannock for dinner, and afterwards, although it was forbidden when they were on the trail, a crock of English brandy. Isobel drank a mouthful, just to warm herself. Such a pleasant feeling, as though she had a wick running through her and that wick had just been lit, as though she glowed—if for only a few minutes. She wanted more; she wanted to belong. Soon they were all boisterous, laughing and singing, building the fire up higher and higher. When the wolves howled, they howled back.

"Gie us a song, lad," they said to her.

"I canna sing."

"Ach, gie us a song just the same."

Watching Scarth from the other side of the campfire, she thought he was not so drunk as the others, was only pretending. It occurred to her for the first time that he might be afraid of her. Could that be?

One of the men handed her the crock. "Come lad, 'tis your turn to entertain us."

She heard Scarth murmur, "Let him be," but she smiled at them all from the centre of her drunkenness, smiled at Scarth in particular, and began a rhyme we used to say as children:

Tell-pie, Picky Fermo

Sat upon a tree;

Knock down aipples

Wan, two, three.

Wan for baby

An wan for the lady

Bit none for the wan

That tells on me.

Finishing up, she gave Scarth another smile. "D'ye remember that, John Scarth, from when you was a laddie?" Then she lay down to sleep.

In the middle of the night she got up to relieve herself, walking away from the fire, which was kept alive because of the cold and the wolves. The men were snoring heavily, even the man who had drawn the short stick and whose job it was to tend the fire in the early hours.

An area around the camp had been well stamped down, but she wished to go a little farther off, where there was no chance she could be seen. There was a hard, bright moon and she wanted to be in shadow.

She had just squatted down when a hand was clamped across her mouth and nose and her head jerked back.

"Hello, Johnny," he whispered.

The whole thing was done silently, just the sound of him as he went in and out, in and out, his breathing, quiet at first and then harsh.

It went on and on; she bit her lip until she tasted blood. On and on—he stopping sometimes, withdrawing a little, slowing himself down; she thinking it was over. And then he would begin again. Finally he came to a shuddering stop.

"Cover yersel' before you freeze," he whispered. "Don't follow me, John. Come back another way."

She nodded, kept her head down, still on her knees. Only after she felt that he was truly gone did she stand up, trying not to whimper. Then, as she stumbled back to camp, she felt she was being watched. There was a figure among the trees, someone moving, keeping pace with her. Not Scarth. She covered her mouth so that the scream could not come out. He stepped forward, nodded to her and disappeared. The Him-Har.

All this told to me, mumbled to me, wept to me, as she sat in the schoolroom, the child asleep, her tears falling on the slate, making a mess of her letters. I was grateful for her downcast face. She was not to know how much her tale had shocked me—the explicitness of it. Shocked and—I am ashamed to say—excited.

"I am so very sorry," I mumbled. She nodded her head; I left her there to collect herself and hurried away. I could stand no more revelations that day.

SHE HAD NOT KNOWN HOW to use an axe when she arrived at the bottom of the Bay. Who chopped wood in our native land? But once she learned, she was good at it, knew just the right angle, chopped steadily and well. After the incident in March, when she chopped she imagined Scarth—*there* went his fingers, *there* his hands, *there* his legs, thud and thud and thud until he was all broken and lying in bits.

"Him doan chop th' tree," said the men of John Fubbister. "Him attacks hid!"

WHEN I HAD BEEN IN THE schoolroom a month, Isobel asked me to teach her to read.

"You have never learnt?"

She shook her head. "Hid didna seem so important back then, but now . . ."

"Why so especially now? To be able to read the letters from your sister?"

"Aye, there's that. But . . ." She waved her hand in the direction of James, who was crawling after a little ball made of scraps of leather and filled with spruce needles. She tossed it gently; James crawled after it and brought it back like a wee puppy dog.

"I dinna want him to be ashamed of me."

"Why should he be ashamed? From what I can see, you are an excellent mother."

"D'you think so?"

"I do."

"I want him to be schooled," she said. "To learn his alphabets and cyphers."

"You have dreams for the boy?"

She nodded. "D'you think me daft?"

"No. Not at all." I hesitated. "Is it your intention to stay here indefinitely?"

I pictured James growing up at Albany Fort. He would have the advantage of being purely white and, if he was as bright as he looked, might well advance in the Company. How much the fact that he was a bastard would hold him back I didn't know. James would speak Cree and English—a great advantage. He might become a first-rate interpreter or even a chief trader, if not a factor. He could certainly become a writer, perhaps a personal secretary. The ability to write clearly and legibly was rare. Mr. Morton told me that last year he had given up on his writer, sent the man away to Moose Factory, and now did all his writing himself. In the scales of advancement at the Bay, would the fact that James was white outweigh the fact that he was a bastard? At the

moment he played quite happily with the half-breed and
Native children; would this still be the case when he was
grown?

And suppose a good position for James came to pass?
What would Isobel's status be? Could she ever be regarded
as anything but a disgraced woman? Even if she told about
Scarth, I was not such an innocent that I did not realize it
would make no difference how men looked at her. And
hadn't she behaved in a most unfeminine fashion in the first
instance, dressing up as a man and pretending to be what she
was not? I knew that the men (not the officers) were fond of
Isobel and some pitied her situation. But I had heard their
talk when in their cups and knew that *au fond*, as Mr. Morton
would say, they wondered if she hadn't got what was coming
to her. She was regarded more highly by the "country gentry"
in the plantation outside the walls than she was by her countrymen within. Within, she was tolerated by all because of
James; there wasn't a man among us whose face didn't
brighten at the sight of that child.

The longer I remained at Albany the more it seemed to
me that there was not much difference between a penal
colony and this life, except of course that the Company's
servants were technically free. But free to go where and
do what? Unless dismissed, they must work out their contracts, serve their time. Were these forts not the northern
equivalents of Van Diemen's Land? (Or Van Diemen's Land
without the two hundred lashes? I had never seen a man
physically punished here.) There was a monotony to the
work of the ordinary labourers; it simply depended on

the seasons what hard task they were put to next. Yet they were not in chains and they chose to come here. And they could—eventually—leave, were encouraged to do so. The Company was not in favour of settlement. It was ridiculous—was it not?—to consider these men prisoners. Why had I ever thought them so? Why did I continue to return to this theme? Because I regretted my own decision? Because I was lonely? Because I did not feel that I belonged? James, and my conversations with Isobel, became the most important things in my life.

Was Isobel afraid that if her son advanced, he would cast her off?

"I will teach you to read and write, if you wish."

"Today?" And then, as an aside, "I'm nivver goin' back."

And so we began with the letter A, big and little. I drew them on the slate.

"A for axe," I said, and was rewarded with one of her rare smiles. "B," I said, "for boat."

She took up a chalk. "A," she repeated. "A."

I wrote "A-X-E" underneath.

"The second letter is an X, but you know that, perhaps?"

"Aye. 'Tis how I make my mark."

"The third letter is an E." I tried to think of a word that would conjure up a picture for her, remembered the figure on the cliff. "E for egg," I said.

Over and over again. A. Axe.

The alphabets sent out by the Scottish Society for the Propagation of Christian Knowledge were well-meaning, but not too useful in practical terms. A for ark, B for Bible.

I had been contemplating an alphabet of my own making, and watching Isobel's delight as she discovered that A was for axe and B was for boat convinced me that the children would benefit from such a book. I would make it large, so that I could stand at the head of the class and show it to all at the same time.

I asked MacNeil if there were any pieces of oiled cloth, such as were used to protect the inland cargo, that I might have for my project. He said he would look in the stores, and the next day he appeared at the flanker with a roll of the waterproof cloth.

"Will this do, Mr. Inkster?"

"This will do very well."

He also provided me with scissors and some vermilion.

We worked on the alphabet book together, the children and I. All of the words came directly from their everyday life. C was canoe and D was deer. The only difficulty was with X. I told them it was the Roman way of writing the number ten, but they looked too puzzled. I opened the Bible and showed them. "You see, it is just another way of numbering." In the end they voted to let X stand alone. The trader's daughter, Harriet, said X was what she did with her fingers when she told a fib.

"Not too often, I hope," said I.

When it came to Z, they were pleased with my story of the striped horse who lived in Africa and was called a zebra.

Once we had decided on the words for our alphabet, I approached Mr. Morton, hoping he might be willing to draw the illustrations.

"I'm sorry, Mr. Inkster, I don't quite understand."

"The children have trouble with the alphabets that were sent out by the sspck, sir, and so I hit upon the idea of making an alphabet that related directly to their life here at the Bay."

He looked at me coldly. "How very clever of you."

"I thought you might help with the illustrations, sir. I am hopeless at such things. I know you are a very busy man——"

He held up his hand. "I think you should use the materials provided, Mr. Inkster. It is not your job to improvise——or at least not when there are excellent materials to hand."

"You do not approve of our alphabet, sir?"

"I do not. Please abandon this project."

I was astonished. I had expected praise for my ingenuity. I wanted these children who had been given under my charge to do well. "Can you tell me why, sir?"

"I have already told you. It is not your job to be clever; you were not sent here to be clever. The society made it very clear that the emphasis is to be on teaching these children to be good Christians. They must learn to read and write, of course. That is a step towards their reading of the Bible. And it may be useful for the boys in terms of the Company and future employment. Not the pure-blood Natives, of course, but the society was firm on that: *all* children at the Bay were to be taught, not just the half-breeds. Ridiculous, but there you are."

"But if an alphabet such as this teaches them quicker, awakens their interest?"

"You are to teach only from texts based on the *sacred*,

Mr. Inkster. This life is profane enough without any help from you." He gathered up the pages on which I had carefully written out our alphabet, with plenty of room for drawings below.

"I admire your enthusiasm, Mr. Inkster, but in this case it is misplaced."

"I disagree."

"Oh, don't do that, sir. That is not wise."

"And what do I tell the children?"

"Tell them that you've changed your mind, that it was not a good idea. Tell them whatever you like. You are good with words; you can think up something. I'll keep these."

Yet the very next day he arrived in the schoolroom with the alphabet under his arm. I wondered what humiliation was in store, but I calmly asked the children to stand and say good morning to the chief factor. He began to quiz them on the catechism, since this is what we had been working on when we were interrupted. The traders' sons and MacNeil's daughter acquitted themselves well, but some of the other children were too shy to open their mouths.

Then he thrust the papers at me.

"I do not approve," he said, "but the doctor, whose judgement I trust, tells me you are a fine addition to our little band at Albany and I am a fool to disallow this. Here."

"Thank you so much."

"I hope the Society never hears of this."

"No, sir."

He turned on his heel and left the room. Since I had not yet thought up a way to tell the children the alphabet was banished, I simply smiled stupidly while they looked on in puzzlement.

But he would not do the illustrations, and every so often at dinner he would make some disparaging remark about my "methods." Since he did not reappear in the schoolroom for many days, I ignored him. And the traders told me separately that they applauded the new alphabet because it "made sense." Each week we added new words on scraps of cloth. B for beaver (of course), C for captain, et cetera. But when Harriet MacNeil suggested R for rum, I shook my head. Even the most enlightened member of the SSPCK would never approve of that one, and who knew what gossip got back to Mr. Morton?

Now, three times a week, after the scholars were dismissed, Isobel came forward from her corner and began her lesson. Gradually, as the weeks went on, she told me bits of her history; I think she needed to talk as badly as she yearned to read and write.

Once or twice Mr. Morton asked why I lingered so long in the schoolroom. When I replied that I prepared each day's lesson from what had been accomplished the day before, he smiled his little smile and congratulated me on my diligence, reminding me that if I used up all the wood allotted to the schoolroom I would find myself out chopping with the others. But he was a very busy man, even as winter drew on (the river froze fast on November 1), and he left me pretty much alone.

F for fort, F for feather, F for fur. James, on his mother's lap, imitating us, "Fuh, Fuh, Fuh."

I held Divine Service on Christmas morning. The world

beyond the fort lay still and silent, locked in a frozen sleep.

It was a simple service; Mr. Morton read the lesson and I gave a short sermon on the concept of God's love and the frozen heart. I had worked very hard on it and hoped my father would have approved. (Mr. Morton said at dinner that he was surprised a Scot could be so "fanciful.") We sang a few psalms, myself acting as precentor, and then my little choir of scholars, whom I'd been secretly rehearsing, gave a sweet if slightly shaky rendition of John Byron's hymn "Jesus shall reign where'er the sun / doth his successive journeys run." The children had some problems with the words, but I had chosen it for its rollicking good tune. I felt that here at Albany Fort we were far enough away from Presbyterian taboos that God would forgive me for encouraging the singing of a hymn as part of Divine Service.

Many of the Natives attended, standing against the back wall, and Isobel sat on a wee stool, in the farthest corner, holding James on her lap. I had been somewhat extravagant with candles, for which I was chided later ("I hope those were from your own supply, Mr. Inkster"), and had gone out the day before to hack a few branches from the snow-burdened trees. Too much decoration would have been popish or pagan or both, but I felt we needed light and greenery to lift our spirits on this day.

James was dressed in cap and coat and mittens made of white rabbit fur, his red curls all the brighter for the contrast. At one point in my sermon, he gave a huge laugh—a crow of delight—and I paused and smiled as all eyes turned to him and Isobel hid her face behind her shawl. When I resumed I could see tears in the eyes of some of the men, who were remembering their own children and families so far away or perhaps were simply moved by the sight of such innocence. In a way, James's laughter was better than any sermon I could preach. Hardened, dour men, eyes prickling from the sound of an infant's laughter.

We had extra rations that day, and gifts of liquor and tobacco were given to the Natives. Arguments broke out.

"Why do you give them liquor?" I asked Mr. Morton over our dessert of nuts and port wine.

"Economics. Practicality. If we don't they won't act as middlemen for the furs, but will desert us for the Canadians or the North West Company. I don't like it, but needs must." He sighed. "We water it down, but it doesn't seem to make a jot of difference."

"We water it down," said the surgeon, "not to save them, but to save money. Let us be honest, please."

Morton shrugged. He pushed a piece of paper across to me. "What do you think?"

It was amazing. It was me to the very life, gripping the lectern with both hands, a lock of my hair, which badly needed cutting, hanging like a dark coil over one eye. It was absolutely true and yet somehow a mockery, almost a caricature. I sensed, rather than saw, a mocking eye behind the artist's hand.

"Very . . . clever," I said.

"It's yours." He smiled and I felt that he had seen through me. Dark-haired I might be, but in truth I was a whited sepulchre.

James's birthday was December 29. I had gone to the
head carpenter, a taciturn man who had been at the Bay for
years. He came from South Ronaldsay and it was said that his
mother became furiously insane, and that one night, when he
was about fourteen years of age, she had gone to his bed and
castrated him. Through some miracle he didn't bleed to
death, and after he was well (his mother safely locked up in
gaol) he left home and made his way across the water to
Mainland, where he became a lad-of-all-work in the harbour
at Hamnavoe. He was found to be clever with his hands and
was eventually apprenticed to a local carpenter. Then, when
he was eighteen, he signed on with the Bay. No doubt there
were many who, for various reasons, saw a life in Upper
Canada as sanctuary. He carried with him everywhere a
cloud of sawdust and wood shavings, and his body gave off
a pungent, resinous smell. I had commissioned him to make
a set of wooden letters, and when I went to fetch them I
was delighted. He had added, as his personal contribution, a
deerskin sack he had obtained from one of the Native
women. I presented this to James at the Christmas gift-
giving and gave Isobel a smile to indicate she was included in
the gift as well. Each letter was about three inches in height
and sanded as smooth as silk, then polished with candlewax.
Now she could practise letters and words whenever she
chose, not waiting to use the precious slates and hornbook,
which I never let out of the schoolroom. Everyone admired
the letters, and Eric, for that was the carpenter's name, was
brought forward to take a shy, embarrassed bow. Several of
the men had made small gifts for the boy—a whistle, a tin

cup, a doll in the costume of a voyageur—for James was a great favourite.

The Scots have never cared much for Christmas festivities. Hogmanay is our winter celebration (first footing observed even at Albany Fort, as I was to discover a few days later), but here it was a boisterous and merry event—to break the monotony of winter—and everyone seemed to benefit from it.

Or almost everyone. As was usual when liquor was flowing freely, fights broke out among the Home Guard. Liquor was poison to them; it horrified me how they changed when under its influence, changed more than white men, or perhaps it just seemed so because normally they were such proud, quiet people. By Christmas night they were all drunk, even the women and children. Most had staggered out into the night when a young woman, I suppose in a fit of jealousy, stuck a gun in her husband's mouth and blew his head apart. Then, before we could stop her, she turned the gun upon herself. Mr. Morton had retired, but the surgeon, whose gout was troubling him sorely owing to his excesses, was sent for and came limping into the hall in a furious temper. All the rest of the Home Guard were chased outside, where they whooped and hollered under the frozen moon, setting off the dogs and, in the forest beyond, the wolves. The bodies of the two young people were fetched by their relatives and taken away for whatever rites and rituals were performed in such cases. Two of the lowest-ranking labourers were ordered to make sure all blood and bits of brain were washed away before daybreak. We went to our various cabbins in a sombre and sober mood.

Four days after Christmas Mr. Morton and the surgeon set off for a visit to Moose Factory ("Shall I give greetings to your fellow schoolmaster?"), leaving the two traders and me to cope with any emergencies that might arise. The paramount chief of the Home Guard had come, in ceremonial dress, for a private interview with Mr. Morton. He was very angry and we had heard him shouting at the surgeon. The young man had been the favourite son of the chief. Everything was resolved, appropriate gifts were given, including a quantity of vermilion for painting the corpses, but the whole affair had put *our* chief in bad humour. He made up his mind to absent himself from Albany until after New Year's Day, and resolved to visit Mr. Murray, the chief factor at Moose. He and the surgeon appeared to have made it up.

"I expect *you*," he said to me, "to keep an eye on things. I have locked up the spirits and taken the key. There will be no drinking and carousing in my absence."

"The men will mutiny, sir," said MacNeil.

"They must be punished for this disgraceful business."

"But it was you, sir, who allowed the giving out of spirits to the Natives."

"But it was the rest of you, *sir*, who stood by and let things get out of hand. You talk of mutiny! The chief of the Home Guard talked of more than that. Please, once and for all, disabuse yourself of the notion that these flimsy matchsticks we call a palisade could keep out an attack if those savages out there had a mind to initiate one. There is also the possibility of them crossing over to our rivals. The chief muttered about that as well. More presents! So fare thee well and have a sober New Year, for once. That should be something to write home about, when next you write a letter."

He turned away, dismissing us, then came back.

"I hope, Mr. Inkster, that you have said a few prayers for their copper-coloured souls?"

How splendid they looked, Mr. Morton and the surgeon, wrapped up in fur rugs in the elegant carioles. The dogs, in their decorated harnesses, stood panting in the moonlight, waiting for the command to "*Marche! Marche!*"

Travelling by night was easier on the dogs, and a third set was fastened to a sledge carrying tent and supplies for stops along the way.

"You can be sure there's plenty of brandy beneath that canvas," muttered MacNeil. "I hope they fall through the ice and drown." He looked at McTavish and me and smiled. "I didna say that."

The command was given, Mr. Morton and retinue set off southward over the frozen river and we turned back through the main gate and across the quadrangle. I could hear cries and lamentations coming from the plantation. The sudden death of those two young people had shaken me profoundly. As though reading my thoughts, MacNeil said, "D'ye think it would have been a better thing, Mr. Inkster, if the white man had stayed home? Better for them over there, I mean. Aye, and mebbe better for us as well. Are we not become the

Devil's servants? God knows they can be vicious enough to their own enemies, but why should we give them instruments to augment their viciousness? Is there much to choose between us, d'ye think? We make mock of their pagan practices, but what do we really worship, if not the beaver?"

He did not require an answer and I gave him none. "Will the men mutiny?" I asked him.

"Of course not. They all have their own secret supplies of whisky, never fear. It's business as usual for Hogmanay."

"Does the governor know this?"

"Probably. He's all blether."

"The bit about the old chief as well?"

"No. Not that. I think the whole affair really shook him. The dead boy was a great favourite. The ties of family are as strong with them as they are with us. Stronger. And the inclination towards revenge. I expect it's been smoothed over. This time."

The Home Guard stayed away from the fort on Hogmanay, even the women who were allowed, by custom, to sleep inside. MacNeil was right about the secret stores of whisky, however, and although I was not the only dark-haired Scot in the Company, far from it, I was prevailed upon to do the honours. And so, bundled against the severe cold (the thermometer that morning had registered forty below zero), I went outside a few minutes before midnight, stamping my feet and slapping my mittened hands against my breast, and waited for the signal—three volleys would be fired on the stroke of twelve—when I would rap hard upon the door and be first across the threshold. I had a piece of charcoal tucked in my mitt instead of a burnt peat or a lump of coal, but it would serve.

After a dram or two with the men, I retired to my small apartment. I did not feel like drinking with the traders or the men and was pierced with a great stab of loneliness. Years later, talking to a young homesick Irish lad, he said he found Edinburgh "scaldingly lonely." That was how I felt at the birth of the New Year. I uncorked my own private bottle, but finding something too awful in the idea of toasting the New Year by myself, I set a candle on my writing table, took down the mirror from the wall and propped it against my few books. There I toasted those dear men, my father and the doctor; I toasted the memory of my beautiful mother; I raised my cup to "absent friends"; I looked in the mirror and toasted the jumping, wavering underwater image that was me.

And then I went to bed. From far away I could hear the sounds of an accordion and fiddle and voices raised in the old songs of our homeland. "Will ye no awa' tae go awa', will ye no . . ."

New Year's Day was still bitterly cold, but brilliant with sunshine and a bright blue, cloudless sky. After breakfast the men brought out their heavy blankets and I was told to do the same. A short while later, wrapped up so heavily I must have appeared more beast than man, and indulging in a pipe outside in the clear air, I was amazed to see the blankets spread out upon the snow and the washerwomen jumping vigorously up and down upon them. It looked like some strange New World ritual, but the carpenter, who was also enjoying his pipe, explained to me that this was how the blankets were washed. In a half-hour they would be as white as new, the snow around having received the dirt and grime of months. The women seemed to be enjoying themselves greatly, calling to one another, laughing, much in the way I imagined villagers in those southern climates enjoyed the trampling of the grapes. Later the blankets would be handed back to their owners (each man had his mark in the corner) and small tokens of appreciation would be given in exchange. The blankets, said the carpenter, dried very quickly on long poles above the stoves.

I did not see Isobel among the jumping women; she was officially my washerwoman, but my blanket had been snatched up by someone else.

In the afternoon those men who had not retired to their cabbins, nursing fierce headaches from the Hogmanay celebrations, cleared snow from a large section of the frozen river and played a game, rather like shinty, with curved sticks and a leather ball. The Native women and their children brought out toboggans and began sledding, starting from a built-up bank and whizzing down, flying across and almost to the centre of the ice. Here, just as I was about to join the men, I saw Isobel, so bundled up I recognized her, at first, only by the smaller bundle on her lap, red curls peeping out from beneath his hood. She waved and beckoned to me to join them. There were a few men from the fort participating, including McTavish, with his country wife and children, so I felt it would not be incorrect to do so. I knocked out my pipe and put it in a deep pocket.

One of the women, acting as steersman, gave me her

place at the back of Isobel's toboggan and away we went. With the first rush of speed I let go of all my melancholy and gave myself up to the pure joy of being a child again. I was with my father and mother, helping to pull a home-made sledge halfway up Ward Hill and then screaming with fear and delight as we hurtled down.

We went down and back and down and back until the first pink streaks of evening appeared in the western sky. On our penultimate run we skidded off course and the toboggan tipped us all out, sprawling, into the snow. Isobel had never let go her grip on James, rolling with him, but when she sat herself up and examined him, laughing, he howled and we could see his wee nose was bleeding. With an application of cold to the back of his neck it soon stopped and his mother rocked him, singing an old rhyme my mother sang to me:

> Davie Dip
> Davie Dip
> Fell i' the fire and brunt his lip
> He's no verry well, but he's
> brawly yet.

Soon the child was laughing and ready for one more ride.

"Will there be school the morn?" Isobel asked as we said our goodbyes.

"No. Not tomorrow. But come the next day if you can."

"Ach, I'll be there—never fear."

All I could see were her eyes, for she spoke through a woollen muffler. I turned towards the gate of the stockade and she turned in the opposite direction.

"Happy New Year," I called.

"And to you."

By September she would be gone.

That evening I thought a great deal about Isobel Gunn. In spite of her childhood and youth—for it seemed to me her life had consisted mostly of darkness, both physical and spiritual—she had a greater capacity for happiness than I. When she sat up out of the snowbank, her long muffler had come loose and the cold made her pitted cheek look even worse, mottled red and blue, but her eyes shone bright and her laugh was the laugh of pure unselfconscious pleasure. Was it the child who had done this for her? She had told me, in one of her "confessions," how horrified she had been when it finally dawned on her that she was carrying Scarth's child. At what point had she put all that behind her—the drunken father, the mad mother, the attack? At the moment of birth or when the blind mouth sought her breast? She, outcast that she was, had friends and a sort of family here; she made the best of things. I had no one. (I ignored the small voice inside me that said, "And whose fault is that?")

THE NIGHT BEFORE JOHN SCARTH died, John Oman, a fellow Orkneyman, had accidentally nicked Scarth's right wrist with a bullet. Oman was cleaning his gun and for some reason—the men said he had mentioned trouble with the breech—fired it off, presumably to test it, just as Scarth was coming back to camp. The two men were part of a group

carrying inland cargo to Martin's Falls. The weather had
turned very bad, with blinding rain and strong winds, so
they decided to make camp a little early, everyone exhausted
and soaked to the skin. Scarth had been acting as steersman,
as usual.

The wrist bone had not shattered, but the wound was
extremely painful and Scarth lost a fair amount of blood. It
was decided the next morning that for that day, at any rate,
he would act as one of the midmen and leave the steering to
someone else.

Unfortunately, the river being quite wild, the canoe ran
up against a rock and a gaping tear meant they had to get
quickly to shore, salvage the goods and make repairs before
continuing. The steersman, seeing a flat rock nearby, gave a
great leap and went from there to land. One of the midmen
did the same, but Scarth, seemingly unafraid or unaware of
the grave danger he was in, was slow to act. The men called
out to him to be quick; they said later he seemed dazed, perhaps from pain or the spirits he had consumed the previous
night when he couldn't sleep.

Almost immediately the canoe spun away from the shore
and was carried out into the middle of the raging river. For
several seconds it seemed to disappear completely and then
it rose up once and sank beneath the surface of the water.
However, Scarth was soon spotted atop a bale of goods,
trying to paddle towards shore with his good arm.

The men called encouragement to him and searched
frantically for a long branch or a vine or anything they could
hold out to him and effect a rescue. Alas, there was nothing

long enough or strong enough, and after a while Scarth floated farther and farther away and then was gone from view.

That night the storm abated; the bales—most of them—floated in to shore, along with several broken pieces of canoe. These they burnt, the rising gum causing them to catch fire easily, even in that wet weather, and saved the nails for another day. Eventually they made their way to Martin's Falls. Scarth's body was never found.

This happened in October 1807; Isobel was six months pregnant at the time but had told no one. Or so I thought until tonight, keeping watch over her body. I am determined to take her small sea-kist with me when I return to Edinburgh, and so I opened it, just to see if there was anything inside. There was the sketch Mr. Morton did of James, all those years ago, and a lock of coppery hair folded up in a small piece of yellowed linen. There was a bundle of letters from me and a few from Nellie Craig. Then, way at the bottom, a receipt, the ink faded nearly to illegibility. "To John Oman, £1.10." Deducted from her first year's wages—and paid out to John's wife by Mr. Geddes. I knew I had heard that name before, and now it has come back to me.

How was it arranged? What made you trust Oman over the other men, or were they all in on it and he the one who took the most risk? As you told me your history, that year at Albany Fort, were there other things you forgot to mention, or only this?

I have put the lock of hair in the back of my watch for the present. I shall get a frame for the sketch and James's hair shall be tucked into the backing. I have replaced my letters and the two letters from Jannet; the second must somehow have made its way back to you. I read Nellie's letters—how happy she was, at first, to be in Edinburgh—and once more my heart ached that she had never contacted me when things began to go wrong. I have consigned the receipt to the candle flame.

And if James should ever appear? Do I tell him what really happened to his father or do I repeat what the men said in their report? Scarth left behind a country wife and four children at the Bay, a wife and three sons in the parish of Firth. To the Company he was a long-time and loyal servant who died an accidental death. His family here received compensation. And there was always that risk—at the Bay—that you might never come home again.

DERE SONE I thot of you on your birth day.

All through the long, hot summer of 1807 the men endured the heat and the sabre-toothed mosquitoes, the gnats that made their ears run with blood.

At night the sound of slaps and curses could be heard from all the cabbins. Is there anything worse than the high metallic whine of a mosquito somewhere in the vicinity of your naked ear? And still, no matter how badly you sleep, there are duties and chores that prevent you from ever lying in.

In late August the ship came in and out, and Isobel felt safer. There was a letter from her "cousin" Jannet, which she took away to the tailor to read, for he had some schooling. It was full of homely gossip and talk of her imminent wedding, how sorely "John" would be missed on the wadding-walk and at the dancing. But they would drink to his health and the health of all the Orkneymen at the Bay. Her closing remarks made Isobel smile: "Doe not fall in love with a indian gearl."

With the help of the tailor, she sent back a brief message with the returning boat, along with a necklace of blue beads she had purchased on Trading Day. How she longed to pour out her heart to her sister, but she held her tongue. It was obvious to her now that she would be discovered, but she would not reveal her identity until she had to. Sometimes the Company censored the men's letters, for they did not want too much talk of the trading aspect of their life. It would be her luck to have Mr. Morton open her letter and send her home immediately. She had worked hard, helping to do up the bundles of furs in parchment, and the sudden inactivity, after the ship had gone and before the laying up of wood and sustenance for the winter began, left her in a dreamy state. She said she felt as though nothing was quite real, and that from now on she would not fight against her fate. Years later, in Edinburgh, I was to hear a condemned prisoner echo those words the night before his hanging: "It's a' a dream from this day forth."

In November, as I have already recounted, she was one of the men sent to Pembinah on the Red River with inland cargo. They were late getting started and would have to stay the winter. The men were relieved to be away from Albany Fort; although it was a long pull to Pembinah, it was also an adventure. At night Isobel did not join in the talk around the fire, but rolled herself into her blankets and fell into a troubled sleep. The child moved vigorously within her most of the day, but it too seemed exhausted by evening and let her rest. The old dream came back, about the forest of hanging women, but it was joined by others, equally terrible, about ships on fire and snarling dogs eating something—bloody paw prints on the snow. Twice she woke up shouting, and the men teased her in the morning. "D'ye have a bloody deed in your past, John Fubbister, that ye cry out so?"

TELLE ME IF YOU ARE raley hapy.

Isobel stood against the wall of the flanker, pretending to be too drunk to want to dance, watching the dancers, Native and white, stamp their feet and holler and prance to an accordion and two fiddles. They cast huge dancing shadows on the walls. Babies were propped up in corners, asleep in their carrying cradles while their mothers danced. "Now!" she willed the child within her. "Now!" But aside from giving her hard kicks, the baby refused to budge. If only she could ask one of the women how to bring it on. If nothing happened this night she would have to go out into the forest and wait; wait and hide, for once she was reported missing they would send a search party. How could she elude them when every stumbling step would be revealed in the snow? Never mind, if she left now she would have a head start, and there were snowshoes stacked up outside. And muskets. She would need a gun to keep away the wolves. And, perhaps, to turn upon herself before they caught up with her. While she imagined herself moving through the forest, doing all these desperate things, she stood still and stared at the shadow-dancers on the walls.

Thus Christmas night passed, and the next day, when the men held their heads and groaned and swore the sun was cruel against the snow. She would have to act before long; the Company men would be heading back to the Company fort as soon as they were able. The forest was the only answer. She would be brave, and if she was brave she would never have to face the ignominy of discovery—or not while she was living. She wished she could send a letter to Jannet, to tell her it was better this way.

But she didn't want to die, not really. It seemed cruel that she had to punish herself for what Scarth had done. She didn't want to die, but she didn't want to go back to being Isobel Gunn. Death seemed a better way out.

Then the pains began. She had not known they would be so fierce, so sudden. She began to yell, and her mates came running.

Even then she did not reveal herself, but her friends, alarmed by her groans, sent a message to Mr. Henry. Could John come into the sitting-room and lie by the fire? She still thought she might deliver the child by herself and hide it somewhere if she could just be left alone. So they helped her into the sitting-room and left her there.

The pain was terrible; she thought the baby was stuck and would kill her trying to get out, shoved the end of her smock in her mouth to keep from crying out.

She lay down by the hearth, and in her distracted state the
flames from the fire became the flames of hell. She was being pun-
ished for her wicked thoughts. She was nearly mad, and screaming,
by the time Mr. Henry came along with the doctor. "What's this?
What's all this racket?"

"And that was th' end of John Fubbister," she said. "In half
an hour the wee boy was born. James.

"Mr. Henry belonged to the Nor' Wast Company, and yet
he was so kind to me, a good, kind man."

"The men in your own Company must have been astonished."

"Aye. And some were not so kind."

"Nobody likes to be fooled."

"'Tis so. But all were kind to James."

At the sound of his name, the child looked up from his
play and smiled.

"How could I have ever entertained the thought of doin'
away with him, Mr. Inkster? How could I?" She buried her
face in her hands, and James, worried, crawled over to her,
tugging at her sleeve. She wiped her eyes and smiled at him.
"Nay, nay," she said. "It's all right, darlin'," then took him in
her arms and smothered him with kisses.

"Sometimes," she said, looking up at me, "he touches my
face—the bad side—but never in a bad way, just curious.
And in my fancy I wonder if his touch might heal me, though
I know in truth it cannot."

"He has healed deeper wounds," I said, and my voice
trembled.

"Aye," she said, "he has that."

As the long winter wore on, I came more and more to feel that my original analogy of the fort as a ship, an analogy I had thought of in physical terms—the creaking of the wood, the cramped living quarters, the rigid schedule of watches and meals, the ringing of bells—was true in other ways as well. Although we did have the freedom to "go on shore," as it were, it was only with our chief's permission and usually to perform some task—hunting, trapping, ice-fishing—dictated by him and of benefit to the Company or to the community at large. In January and February the days were very short; the sun rose three hours after we had finished breakfast and set three hours after dinner. The thermometer was measuring its lowest temperatures, and the human spirit seemed to darken and freeze as well. I once again thought of penal colonies, and our "ship" was a convict ship and we had all been transported to a northern equivalent of Van Diemen's Land, for could not hell be thought of as heaven's antipodes and did not Dante picture the centre of hell as a block of ice?

Men drank and became maudlin or drank and became violent, even the carpenter, that mildest of men. A young lad from Stronsay actually tried to burn the place down one night and, discovered setting a candle flame to a huge pile of kindling and lint, had to be restrained in a quickly manufactured straitjacket, so outraged was he at being hindered from his plan. The surgeon gave him enough laudanum to keep him quiet for days, but even when he woke up he remained violent and was confined in an empty store-cupboard that was quickly fitted with an opening for ventilation. His

screams and curses were heard for a week, until one day he
got loose when his supper was shoved in through the door,
ran out of the fort and barefoot along the frozen river in the
dark of a moonless night; next morning he was discovered to
have fallen through a fishing hole. His dead eyes looked up at
his rescuers through a thin film of ice. This event cast a further gloom upon the men.

My young scholars were affected by the darkness as well.
They became lethargic, uninterested in spelling and mathe-
matics—all but Isobel Gunn, who went at her letters and
numbers as though they were made of meat and she was
starving. Sometimes Mr. Morton would favour us with a
visit, quizzing the children on this or that and then standing
for a few minutes watching Isobel, or rather, watching Isobel
and James, for his eye was as often drawn to the child as to
his mother.

Our post-prandial conversations began with a glass of
cognac and then some fact about the beaver—"This is the
season of mating for the beaver, Mr. Inkster, were you aware
of that?" or "Beavers do not hibernate, Mr. Inkster, but
remain active in their lodge and beneath the ice." His
Castorologia was growing, and once he had arranged the pages
in their proper order the tailor was to be commissioned to
sew them together and create a cover from a nice piece of
dressed deerskin. I asked if he was going to include any of his
drawings, and he said only those of the skull and skeleton and
a longitudinal view of an adult male. I did not ask what
would happen to the book once completed. No doubt he
would carry it back to London with him, for he made no

secret of the fact that London was where he intended to live once he left the Bay. This was his fourth year, his second at Albany Fort. Three more years—his uncle had promised—and he would be among the passengers boarding the sloop for the *Prince of Wales*.

"What then?"

"London, Mr. Inkster. Civilization."

"Yes, but what will you do?"

"Oh, I shall still be involved with the Company, but in a London capacity. I expect I shall be put in charge of the auction rooms."

I began to laugh.

"Forgive me, but what is so amusing?"

"Forgive *me*, sir, but I had thought, somehow, that you would wish to get clean away from beaver pelts."

His face changed. "If I had a free choice, I would choose never to have anything more to do with beavers, but I am not free—not so long as my mother lives and my uncle is my chief means of advancement."

"Will you continue to draw?"

"Why do you ask?"

"I suppose I was thinking of the parable of the five talents."

"Ah, I see. Yes. Well, I expect I shall hide my talent under a bushel of Made Beaver. But we all have our vices, our guilty pleasures. The surgeon's is drink and laudanum; mine is sketching. What is yours, I wonder?"

"Poetry," I said.

"Indeed? The writing of poetry, Mr. Inkster?"

"No, no. I have no talent in that direction. The reading of poetry."

"Should a man of the cloth be reading poetry, Mr. Inkster?"

"A man of the cloth, Mr. Morton, should be reading anything that gives insight into the human heart. Do you know Dante's disquisition on the 'beautiful lie'?"

"No, and let us save that for another time." He pushed the cognac bottle towards me. "Do you enjoy teaching?" he asked.

"I do. Although I think I learn more than my pupils."

"How so?"

"One has to start at the very beginning with most of these children. Several, when they came to me, did not even know their alphabets. I tended to get impatient, to think they were deliberately obtuse. How can a boy of twelve not know his letters! How can a bright little girl tell me that T-R-E-E spells 'fort'? And then I remembered my own first attempts at Greek, how frustrated I felt—foreign languages do not come easily to me—and I had the very best of teachers, my father, who loved the language and was a man of great enthusiasm and infinite patience, and my professor at St. Mary's. I am slowly learning patience, both big P and little p, Mr. Morton, and I am also devising ways to interest the children, so that basic learning becomes less of a chore."

I told him how the other children had been fascinated by James's gift of the wooden letters and how I had commissioned the carpenter to make a duplicate set for the schoolroom, with a few extra vowels. Each child had a chance to

make a word or two and show it to the class. It seemed to
have mitigated, to a certain extent, their winter doldrums.

"And what do you think of little James? Is he absorbing
anything as he plays there on the floor?"

It is a superstition in Orkney that it is dangerous to praise
someone, especially a child. Praise can call down bad luck.
I answered, therefore, somewhat reluctantly. "I'm sure he is.
He seems a very intelligent child." And added to myself, as
we do, "God bless him."

"Do you really think so?"

"I do."

"Very intelligent?"

"He's only a baby yet, but yes, he strikes me as such."

"And yet he grows up a savage, living in a smoky wiki-
wam with other savages. Did you know they sleep naked,
Mr. Inkster, men and women both? And even in the daylight
hours the women wear no underclothing."

"He does not seem a savage to me, sir, but a very bright
and loving child. His mother looks after him very well."

"Ah, yes, his mother. She may well be a dab hand at keeping him clean and warmly dressed, but what about his moral
education? She is barely above a savage herself—an illiterate
peasant who ran around barefoot most of the year, and when
she became a woman showed her contempt for society and
God's law by disguising herself as a man and following her
lover to the Bay. What kind of a person is that to bring up a
child like James?"

"His mother. She loves him."

"'His mother. She loves him,'" he repeated in a mocking,

falsetto voice. Then, "If she loves him, I imagine she wants what's best for him."

"I'm sure of it."

He changed the subject back to beavers. Did I know that the beaver spent most of his leisure time grooming his pelage? Did I think our servants could learn a lesson from this? Lately they all resembled shaggy-maned beasts.

I thought that my defence of Isobel as a good mother had softened Mr. Morton somewhat, for now when he came to the schoolroom he took the trouble to smile at her and speak kindly to her. James was talking a bit—words in Cree as well as English—the usual simple words a child begins with: Mama, ball, James, me, me, me. He called me Magus. Isobel didn't understand why that amused me, so I explained.

"I dinna want him to call you by your Christian name, even if he gets it right. 'Tis disrespectful."

"I don't mind."

She shook her head. "I do."

She never called me Magnus, only Mr. Inkster. Even when she had revealed to me the most intimate details of her past life, she continued to refer to me in this formal manner. I had thought at first it was because I was the schoolmaster, but one night it came to me that she didn't see me as a man, perhaps not even a human being on the same order as herself. I was always the minister, the man of the cloth. After the New Year's Day tobogganing I thought our friendship would deepen, become more relaxed, but no. All her warmth went towards her son and her friends among the Home Guard, especially an older woman named Mary, who was one of those who shared the same tent.

Years later I discussed this with the minister at Leith, an elderly man with whom I had forged a strong friendship. He said that this had happened to him many times over his long life. He wondered if women of our religious persuasion weren't secret papists at heart, needing to confess to a man, but only to a man stripped of all carnal intention towards them, a man who would listen as a woman might, yet had the authority to absolve and forgive. She was more relaxed with the other Orkneymen at the fort—and some had known her as John Fubbister as well as Isobel Gunn, surely an embarrassing situation?—but even with them she kept her distance, using James as a kind of shield against any real intrusion on her privacy. Yet she trusted me, not them, with her story. So the old minister at Leith was probably right. She confessed to me because I was God's representative at Albany Fort, and she very much wanted God's forgiveness. I didn't have the heart to tell her that I, too, knew something about disguise.

Was James as bright as I thought? I had no experience of babies, but he did seem to me to be exceptionally quick and clever. He was also a very merry child and was very much the mascot of all at the fort, both within and without. In that dark winter we seemed to bend to him as to a flame, warming ourselves on his smile and his innocent laughter.

The most hardened, cynical men spent hours whittling him geegaws or found some excuse to lift him high in the air until he shrieked with pleasure. Drunk or sober no man, except Mr. Morton and occasionally the surgeon, referred to him as Scarth's bantling. In my more reflective moments I wondered what his life would be like if he and Isobel were sent back to Orkney. I had seen enough poor children—indeed, Isobel herself as a child—to know that the life of the poor in our islands was very hard. And I knew this only from the outside, from glimpses, as though I had stood in sunlight, peering into the half-opened door of a windowless house, just barely able to make out the objects in the gloom within.

And yet.

At kelp-making time back in Orphir I had seen nothing but the heavily laden women with their dripping caisies on their backs, their swollen fingers, but Isobel told a different story.

"When I were a wee girl," she said, "we loved to boil eggs in a kettle over the kelp-fire or roast tatties, when we had them, in the ashes. That were grand. Or make seggie-boats and sail them."

She smiled as she said this; to her, at any rate, her childhood was not one of unrelieved gloom. (And had I not seen her myself, emerging triumphant over the cliff's edge, her sling full of hard-won eggs?) But there was, nevertheless, more dark than light in her story—the mother's terrible breakdown, the hunger and cold, the father's drunken curses, Scarth's brutal act.

Later, when I had seen more of the world, had moved among the poor in the dreadful slums of Edinburgh's Old Town, it seemed to me that the rural poor, all things considered, had a much better time of it than the poor of the cities, crowded together, sometimes fifteen or twenty to a room, and with opportunities for vice in every darkened close or wynd. At least, when outside, the poor children of the country breathed air that was pure and fresh.

Perhaps Isobel and James would be all right. Even if her annual stipend had been reduced from six pounds to one pound, and I hadn't asked if this was so, she would still have money owing her when she landed at Stromness. Then there was Jannet and her husband; they would never let her starve. Although I knew she wanted to stay in Rupert's Land "forever," I also knew Mr. Morton was more and more convinced that he should send her away. Rules were rules, he said, and recited by heart the Company's interdiction against allowing white women at the Bay.

By keeping her here he was jeopardizing his own career, he said, for he was deliberately flaunting the rules. "And let us suppose that she undertakes a marriage with one of our men or, worse still, one of the Home Guard—don't smile at me, Doctor, it could happen—what is already a complicated situation becomes even more so . . . becomes untenable!"

"She has shown no inclination towards either of these options," I said. "Her life appears to be dedicated to her son. Her behaviour is never anything but modest."

"Thus far, Mr. Inkster, thus far. But she refuses to live in the fort, does she not? And when her chores here are done, she hurries back to her copper-coloured friends. What sort of impression do you suppose that makes on the child? Any day now I expect to see her coming across the courtyard smoking a clay pipe! No doubt she and the boy sleep naked, like the rest of them. Native women have no modesty, Mr. Inkster. They think nothing of bathing in the river naked and then sitting on the bank, combing each other's hair, laughing and chattering like monkeys until they are dry. Then they walk back, their clothes under their arms, never deigning to cover those parts that should be seen only by their husbands and God. No shame at all."

"Why should they be ashamed," said the doctor, "when to them all this seems completely natural? It's you should be ashamed, sir, for peeking. What is that bit about Susannah and the Elders? From the Apocrypha, I think."

I looked at the doctor with new interest, but Mr. Morton ignored him.

"Perhaps you could include a few words about modesty, Mr. Inkster, in one of your Sunday services? Or even a brief discussion in the schoolroom. I'm sure the SSPCK expects you to do more than teach the alphabet to these children."

O MY DEARE O MY DEARLING I wish we ware to ger wane deay; it makes my hart to bet and my eay to wepe when i think on you.

Although she had dangled from cliffs and guided a plough and carried over her shoulders more weight of water than most men could manage, Isobel had never fired a gun until she arrived at the Bay. The Hudson Bay gun was especially made for the Company in England, and one of its distinguishing features was a brass dragon at the opposite side of the stock from the lock. At first one might think some more northern creature would have been more appropriate, but dragons, not beavers or buffalo, breathe fire, so no doubt that's where the original gunsmith got his fanciful idea. Or perhaps the designer was an Orkneyman; we had dragons in our Viking history, from the dragon-headed ships to stories about Fafnir and his golden hoard. Through two holes in the dragon went the bolts that held the stock to the lock. The gun itself was heavy and clumsy and apt to misfire.

She said it took her a long time to use the powder flask properly, managing the lever so that just the right amount of powder was released, to take the ball from the bag, place it on a scrap of flannel on the muzzle, push it in. She learned to patch the ball, insert the ramrod and push the ball down until it was firmly sitting on the powder. To pull back the cock and lever until—click!—the weapon was on full cock.

The men laughed at John Fubbister's clumsiness and this might have led to suspicion, except for the fact there were others who had never used such an awkward gun—or any gun—before coming out to the Bay. Slingshots were much more the customary weapon for the lads of Orkney.

The first time she actually shot something—a goose— and it fell down from the sky in a blizzard of feathers, she was so pleased with herself she gave a wild whoop, like an Indian, and this made the men laugh even harder.

"D'ye have yer mouth all waterin' for roast goose, Johnny?"

She went to pick it up, but they shook their heads. The Native women plucked the geese, selling the feathers or making feather-beds for the men and keeping back some of the quills for decoration.

She could soon load and reload with the best of them, firing two or three times in one minute. She told me all this with great pride one afternoon, out past the plantation, after watching my pathetic efforts. Later she pulled out from the pile of wooden letters the G. "G for gun," she said, giving me one of her rare smiles. "You'll learn." Mr. Morton had taken her gun away from her now that she was a woman—a white woman. "But I have another," she said, "for emergencies."

"What sort of emergencies?"

She just smiled again and shrugged.

Now in her sea-kist I find a powder-horn, still with some remnants of black powder inside. Someone had made it for her and burnt in her name, then blackened it:

JOHN FUBBISTER
HIS GUNN

For an Indian to get a trading gun he had to pay the equivalent of ten Made Beaver. There was no bargaining for items like this, although credit could be, and usually was, given.

Hundreds and hundreds—thousands—of geese were needed to get us through the winter. During the times of migration, men were sent to the goose tents until the geese had disappeared. Why didn't the geese learn? If they could fly thousands of miles each year, knowing exactly when to leave and where to go, why couldn't they learn to avoid the hunters? A few miles to the east or west and they would have been safe. The leaders, presumably older geese, experienced geese, could have directed them out of harm's way. But no, they kept coming and coming and glad we were of the meat when winter locked us up in our frozen world. Nevertheless, since patterns of behaviour could be learned, even in the animal world—since not all behaviour was instinctual—this bothered me.

"You ponder this because you have a large brain," said Mr. Morton. "The brain of a goose cannot accommodate change—it's too small and simple." A few days later, after dinner, he unwrapped something from a napkin and handed it to me. "There," he said, "do you think there is room inside that thing for decision-making?" He sighed. "Perhaps it is easier to have such a brain; decision-making is wearisome." And thus he brought the conversation around, once again, to the problem of Isobel and her son.

I never told Isobel that I had seen her twice before that autumn day in the schoolroom. The first occasion, when her mad mother was led away without a backward glance, seemed too horrible and too intimate to reveal myself as having been witness to, and the second, when she was cliff-walking, seemed too trivial to mention. I waited—and not in vain—for her to tell me her story herself. It did not come out as a continuous narrative, but in short bursts, or "scenes," which I had to fit together later. These confessions occurred after her lesson, while James played on the floor with one or another of his toys. After an hour of watching her struggle to read the simplest sentence, it was almost a shock to realize how fluent she was when talking. I was reminded of a deaf lad I had known at school; his speech was all grunts or almost unintelligible words. He had no idea where to put the stresses, you see, and he seemed to be speaking from the interior of a cave—which I suppose, in a way, he was. Yet this same boy wrote a beautiful hand and could obviously read and comprehend anything you put in front of him. It was that sort of shock. And she used a lot of the old words that I, with my superior education, had put aside. There were days when I could have listened to her voice forever. She had also picked up many of the Native words since her arrival, and it occurred to me that she herself would make a good inter- preter, a role assigned to Native women at most of the camps. (This was one of the advantages of a trader having a country wife, especially if she was quick at learning the English words for common trading goods: "gun," "kettle," "knife," "blanket," "rum.")

I found Mr. Morton, the surgeon and the two traders less than ideal company (I'm sure they felt the same about me), and I came more and more to look forward to my time with Isobel. Once the river had set fast and winter came, my life often seemed as blank and bleached as the world out- side. We had winter in Orkney, of course, but never a winter that began in late October and carried on to the middle of May. The wind howled around the doors and blew its chilly breath in every crack and crevice in the walls. We burned wood at what seemed to me, coming from such a treeless place, an alarming rate. The dogs howled as well—and the wolves.

One night in February a female dog was killed by a wolf; our cook found the frozen corpse outside the kitchen door.

The dog's neck had been bitten nearly in two. The doctor, who had examined the corpse before it was thrown outside the stockade, asked me at dinner if I could guess why the bitch had died. This seemed so obvious to me I was sure it was a trick.

"Just a fight, I imagine, over food?"

"Not at all. They were stuck together, Mr. Inkster. The wolf killed the bitch in order to get free. It happens from time to time."

"I see," I said with some embarrassment. I couldn't understand where this conversation was heading, but the doctor had a vulgar streak.

"I doubt that you do see," he countered. "Do you know anything about the mating habits of dogs vis-à-vis wolves?"

"I assume they would be roughly the same."

"Oh, roughly, they are. But a female dog contracts against the penis of the male, to hold it in place, while the seminal fluid dribbles out. It is necessary that she do this, necessary and instinctual. With a wolf it is a different matter. The wolf mounts, ejaculates forcefully and it's all over. The wolf in this case must have been frantic when he found he couldn't get away; he had to kill her before she would relax. It can be fatal to mix the species, can it not, Mr. McTavish, Mr. MacNeil?" MacNeil turned a dark red. "At least," added the doctor, "our little resident bastard is purely white."

I felt sickened by the smiles on the faces of Mr. Rooney and the chief factor. They had enjoyed making me uncomfortable; they had enjoyed baiting the traders. At the remark about James, Mr. Morton, who had been leaning back in his chair with his eyes closed, sat forward and stared at me, watching my reaction.

I felt an anger out of all proportion to the "lesson" and the subsequent remarks. I said goodnight abruptly and retired, only to lie awake most of the night, trying to see what the future might hold. I was thirty-one years old, and although I had always prided myself on being solitary by nature as well as circumstance, I knew in my heart I wanted a choice; I did not want solitariness and the single state to descend upon me like a mantle. I could remember what a mother's love felt like, and God knows my dear father loved me and let me know it, but I had never been loved by a woman other than my mother, had not shared even a sister's love. I was quite a presentable specimen; how had I let myself slip so easily into this bachelor role? I had been in the company of boys and men since my school days, but my fellow students at St. Andrews had sisters and cousins, some very pretty, some plain, all decidedly female. I had met many of these girls when they came to visit or when I made the occasional visit to their brothers during the holidays. Some had smiled at me; one had even mentioned, in passing, that she hoped to be a missionary, as was her dear brother's intention. I said something awkward—that I couldn't imagine, even for the love of God, going away from Scotland unless I was forced to—something priggish and stupid like that. I did not have a natural gift for pleasantries, which was surprising, given my talkative and charming parents. I would never go away from Scotland? Indeed! And here I was at the Bay. By the time I returned to Orkney, I would be thirty-six years old and no doubt even more awkward in speech and manner. Even with the surfeit of women at home, owing in part to the very Company I worked for, as well as to the navy and the men who fished the Davis Strait, what woman would look twice at me? In those dark hours I resented my father and the doctor for encouraging me in this course, but at least I had the good sense to absolve them before I fell asleep.

WORK IS SCARC AND bad paed for.

I learned to use snowshoes and took great pleasure on Saturday afternoons, when school was dismissed early, in striding over the snow. Isobel had told me that snowshoes made her feel like a bird, for the birds had the gift of walking on the top of the snow, not sinking up to the knees as happened to us in our ordinary footwear. Occasionally Mr. Morton invited me to join him on a sketching expedition; the carpenter had built him a very clever little easel with adaptable legs that fitted together, pieces screwed in according to the depth of the snow. I did not like the man any better, but I admired his artistic ability and marvelled at how still he could stand, bundled into his heavy outerwear, how quickly he could sketch a fox that suddenly appeared at the edge of the wood, a dead rabbit in its mouth. Mr. Morton had a special mitt for his right hand, with an outer layer that could be turned back so his fingers, in a knitted underglove, could remain free without the danger of frostbite. He had put aside his *Castorologia* until the spring, but he executed one or two fine drawings of the outside of a beaver dam in winter, explaining to me how the Indians cut a hole in the ice downstream from the lodge, set a net, then banged on the top of the apartment itself until the beavers fled outside and were killed.

Sometimes—often—he asked me about Isobel Gunn and I told him how well she was doing. I said there was no doubt she was as intelligent as her son appeared to be. I mentioned, casually, that she might make a good interpreter.

"Hmnn," he said, taking up a piece of charcoal and beginning a sketch of two men, away to the middle of the frozen river, ice-fishing. "She's not so intelligent that she didn't get caught out."

I bit my tongue. I had promised I would say nothing about the rape.

"Of course, we don't know the entire history of that, do we?"

"My dear fellow, what is there to know? She was nothing but a sort of camp-follower in disguise."

I felt I must defend her. "If that were really so, sir, why has she not 'followed' another man now that Scarth is dead?"

He thought about that for a minute. "An interesting point. However, she now has the child to consider—and she has employment with us."

"Would either of those things stop a loose woman? I think not." I was on dangerous ground here; I knew nothing except hearsay about so-called loose women and what they might or might not do.

"You admire her then, Mr. Inkster?"

"I think," I said sincerely, "that I admire her courage. She is trying to make the best of a bad bargain, and for her child's sake she strives to improve herself. And anyone can see she loves the child."

Mr. Morton had dismantled his easel and packed it away in a clever little packsack he carried on his back. We headed towards the fort, our snowshoes making leathery sounds on the hard snow, our breath like smoke.

"What shall we do about the child, Mr. Inkster? Any ideas?"

I did not need to reply, for just at that instant we came across the tracks of a great bear, most unusual, for the hibernation period was not yet over. Mr. Morton quickly turned back his outer mitt, pulled a small sketch-pad from his pocket and knelt down in the snow to examine the tracks more closely. When he stood up, he seemed to have forgotten about his question: What shall we do about the child?

I WISH I WAS BE side you now.

There is a saying in Edinburgh that you can always tell an Orkneyman as he walks along Princes Street, for he will be bent nearly double, like an old dame with a dowager's hump, a result of the fierce winds that scour our islands. It is true that an Orkney blast can, quite literally, blow you from one end of the street to the other, but as for cold—well, I do not think I had ever experienced cold in Orkney like the cold that came in off the North Sea at St. Andrews. (Of course, I had not yet been to the Bay.) Not just icy fingers finding their way up sleeves or trouser legs, down collars, but icy fingers with knives for fingertips. When I had finished my undergraduate work at St. Salvator's and traded my heavy gown of scarlet wool for the thin black gown marking me as a divinity student, I felt the cold most keenly and added yet another layer to my dress. I had no mother to knit for me, but I blessed the doctor's wife, who had equipped me with more than one heavy gansey before I left home, as well as a muffler that could have swaddled a mummy. And how I pitied the two Highlanders among us, whose bare knees turned an angry purple colour in winter, as though they quite literally fell on their knees so often, in their pious zeal, that they bore permanent bruises.

St. Andrews, by the time I matriculated, had come down in the world from the days when it held ecclesiastical primacy. Its cathedral and castle were mere picturesque ruins on a grassy hill, and the student body was in decline. At St. Mary's there were fewer than twenty of us, most living in cupboard-sized rooms in the quadrangle, always shivering, always hungry, always (or nearly always) studying: systemic theology, Hebrew, the Old and New Testaments, ecclesiastical history. The professor of divinity at the time was Dr. George Hill, a "moderate" who was opposed to reform of any kind. He was not a bad teacher; he published his lectures and we pretty well knew them off by heart. But he was very keen to advance the members of his own family. Indeed, there were so many Hills connected with the university that

the students maintained that the most important psalm was
No. 121, "I to the Hills will lift mine eyes!"

What I most remember about that time, however, is the
intense loneliness I felt, so far away from the sights and the
familiar accents of home. I was but fifteen years old when
I went up to university, and a very young fifteen. There were
boys much younger than I was, but I was from the farthest
away. My accent was mocked, even by a lad from Inverness,
whom I thought was speaking a foreign language, possibly
German, the first time we met. The very words I used were
ridiculed, and they laughed heartily at my "fither" instead of
"fah-ther." I knocked a boy down when he asked me what my
"mither's" name was and was taken before the disciplinary
Committee.

In spite of the rough and tumble of my years at school,
I really wasn't very comfortable in groups of boys. In groups
of any kind. The one advantage I had was the fact that I was
good at Greek, in which I had received excellent instruction,
so I was accepted, in the end, because I could tutor others
who had not been so fortunate. Gradually I made a few
friends.

St. Andrews, although not large, was the biggest town
I had ever seen, apart from a brief stay in Aberdeen on my
way down—two days with my mother's family, who were
polite but distant; I'm sure they felt that if my mother had
not chosen to live in Orkney she might still be alive. When I
was not engaged in my studies, I took long walks along the
Scores or, on a sunny day, might sit on the grass below the
ruined castle, wrapped in my gown, reading a book or just

gazing out to sea. I can't remember when first I began to take an interest in Shakespeare, but the doctor, along with a small kist of potions and powders that were guaranteed to keep me healthy if I followed his instructions, had added a well-worn leather-bound copy of the plays. "Another sort of remedy," he said, and winked at me. The book's cover falsely proclaimed that it was *The Good Effects of Prayer* by a Reverend Scott. I can still see myself, a gangly, dark-haired lad, awkward around the arms and legs, climbing the grassy slope and then, settling my robe around me, taking out the precious book and opening it to *The Tragedy of Macbeth*. *Macbeth* was just the thing to read in such a place. By the time my undergraduate years were up, I had read the entire book.

People have asked me since if I knew Thomas Chalmers. Of course I did; everyone knew him, the young prodigy from Anstruther whose amazing gift with words could actually make you believe in the power of prayer. On Prayer Day, when it was Chalmers's turn to preach, the chapel was full to bursting, for his reputation soon extended to the town as well. Prayers were a major part of our life; we attended each day at 9 a.m. and 7 p.m., and on Sundays we attended the town church, sitting in the college loft.

In many ways we were as cloistered as a group of monks, for the gates were shut at 9 p.m. every night and we were expected to behave, at all times, in a sober and industrious manner, to "shun even the appearance of evil." For some reason, my afternoons on the slope beneath the castle were never called into question, perhaps because I was such a good student. I kept my Shakespeare locked in my kist and

my Bible prominently displayed. It had been my mother's
Bible and I treasured it.

Thomas Chalmers was a member of the Political Society
and one day he stopped me as I made my way along Market
Street. I hadn't realized he even knew my name, but now he
said he had heard "good things" of me and invited me to join
the society. Perhaps I might even wish to join in some of the
debates? I said I would consider it and thanked him for
asking. As we parted, he said, "What is the book I saw you
reading up there on Castle Hill?"

"*The Good Effects of Prayer*," I lied.

"It must be immensely absorbing; you seemed oblivious
to the world. May I have a look?"

What could I do? I handed it over and he opened it.
Turned the pages. Handed it back with a smile.

"Shall I hope to see you, then, Tuesday week?" No mention was ever made of my deceit.

Chalmers and I did not become intimate. I liked him
enormously (also envied him, not just for his genius at ora-
tory, but for the fact that he was one of nine children and
lived so close to home). Yet I myself was not politically
inclined. I was too inward-looking to care much about the
rest of the world's woes, this in spite of my parents. However,
their politics was not something derived from any system; it
was simply the politics of piety and compassion, and they
practised it in a small community that had, except for the
lairds, many of whom lived elsewhere, a common culture.

Chalmers, too, was kind and compassionate and wanted
to better the lives of labourers, but he also defended the

doctrine of predestination, so essential to our Presbyterian faith. I cannot say exactly when I began to have doubts, and perhaps if Chalmers hadn't been so eloquent on the subject I might never have started to think for myself. I knew a little bit about Eastern religion, and it seemed to me it was as ludicrous as the idea of the transmigration of souls to declare that, from birth, our spiritual destinies were preordained. And if so (and if we were not working out sins from some past life), on what basis were the elect elected and the damned damned? I longed to debate this with him, but I was too shy. Besides, I wanted to be ordained; everyone expected it of me, and how could I let them down? My father, the doctor, even the doctor's wife, with her wonderful knitting—not to mention my professors, who regularly nodded approval of my efforts although I was, from time to time, warned about the sin of pride. And so I held my tongue, but my heart was troubled.

In the long summer holidays, when students went down, I obtained a post as tutor to the sons of Lord Pitmillie and removed to his elegant estate not far from Dundee. In the bosom of this arrogant household I learned a great deal about pride—it became a dietary staple, for I swallowed it with nearly every meal. The only saving grace was the library, where I was allowed to read, providing my duties were finished for the day. It was there that I discovered the works of Dante (with the pages still uncut) and an Italian-English dictionary. Dante wrote in his native Tuscan, but I persevered.

I completed my studies at Divinity Hall in 1798 and

returned home to be examined by the presbytery covering the Orkney Isles. Lord Pitmillie, who could not help noticing my obsession with Dante, gave me an edition of the *Commedia Divina* as a farewell present. I thought perhaps I had misjudged him, but still I was delighted to be leaving the county of Fife and heading home. I added the Dante to my little library and began the long journey north to Orkney.

I WOLD CROUSE THE ROARING *mane for you.*

Mr. Morton called Isobel for an interview. Her heart was banging against her ribs.

"Isobel Gunn."

"Sir."

He saw in front of him a tall, plain woman with a damaged face. What a pity that glorious hair was wasted on such a creature. She wore it in two plaits, like the Native women, and it looked as though she dressed it in grease, but nothing could completely hide its beauty. She was taller than he was, so he asked her to be seated. Yes, that was better. He remained standing.

"Isobel Gunn, I'm at a loss as to what to do with you. You don't belong at the Bay."

"I can work hard, sir. I cause no trouble."

"Your very presence causes trouble." (Imagined writing in the journal: "This day discussed with the woman Is. Gunn her return to Orkney on the next ship." He could leave out his plans for the boy

until a later date.) "I'm afraid I must dismiss you. You will return home in September."

"Could I no stay here, sir? My life is here now."

"You don't belong here. You used trickery to get yourself here in the first place and we have been kind to you since your discovery, but Company rules are Company rules. No white women at the Bay. You have to go."

"I am the same as when I was John Fubbister an' you praised me for my labour."

"No, you are not the same. It is not seemly for you to work here even if you had the strength of twenty men. Why, if we let you stay all sorts of strong, mannish women would be donning trousers and changing their names—hordes of girls-in-disguise would descend upon us. Unthinkable, Mrs. Gunn, unthinkable! It is hard enough to keep order at these posts without hordes of lassies signing on."

"I dinna think you'd get hordes of lassies, Mr. Morton."

"No? You came, didn't you? Do you think you are unique, one of a kind?"

"Mebbe." She looked him in the eye.

"Hmmn. Humility doesn't seem to be one of your virtues. You are the only one to try this so far, but that doesn't mean it mightn't be tried again. I have to set an example, not a precedent. You will remain in your present occupation as nursemaid and washerwoman, but when the ship comes in I must send you back to Orkney."

And then, clearing his throat, fussing with the papers on his desk, he spoke to her of James. "James is a very bright lad."

"Aye." Careful not to praise him overmuch and call down bad luck upon him, she added, "I suppose."

"Oh, very bright. It's there for all to see." He paused. "And of course you want what's best for him."

"I do, that." She was puzzled but not afraid. He had praised her son, called him "very bright."

"It might be best if I adopted him and brought him up as my son."

He could have been speaking a foreign tongue, it made so little sense. She was speechless.

"Mrs. Gunn, I would like to adopt James, become his legal father. Of course the papers would have to be filed in London and it would take——"

"You?" She shook her head to clear it. The man was daft, surely.

"Why should that astonish you? I shall be returning to London in a few years, and James would go with me, away from all this." He gestured in the direction of the "savage" world outside the palisade.

"No," she said.

He looked at her, as dumbfounded as she had been a minute before. "What do you mean, 'No'?"

"I mean what I say."

"But my dear woman, surely a mother's best wish for her child is that he should grow and prosper in this world."

"Aye."

"Then aren't you being more than a little selfish to deny your child such an opportunity? He will have an excellent education, and with his good appearance and pleasing manner, he should go far."

She knew in her heart the answer, but still she had to ask: "Would you be thinkin' of takin' me as well?"

"Taking you?"

"Aye. His mither. To London."

There was a long silence and then, "No. I had thought of him starting afresh. A new life."

"I suspected that was your thought, sir. Then my first answer must stand. Thank you——but no. James will be all right with me." She turned to go.

"Just think about it," he called to her retreating back.

The next day she came to the schoolroom with the scholars, but without James. After the children had been dismissed, she told me what had taken place the night before.

"He mentioned nothing of this to me—nothing."

"Do you think I was wrong to say no?"

"I think you were quite right."

"I want James to prosper, I do, but he is all I have; I canna let him go."

"Nor should you. I will speak to him myself."

Morton raised his eyebrows when I asked for an explanation.

"Surely it's as plain as the nose on your face. I wish to adopt the boy and make him my son."

"And abandon Isobel Gunn?"

"Let us call it relieving her of a burden she will find more and more difficult to bear. How is she to find food and lodging for herself and the boy in Orkney? What skills does she possess?" He smiled. "I suppose she might go on the stage; she is certainly very clever at disguise and she has no reputation to think of. The boy could sleep in a trunk, perhaps."

"You are intending to send them away?"

"By the next boat, yes. Not 'them,' but Isobel Gunn.

I intend for the boy to stay here—with me." Then he added, "Just what is your interest in all this, Mr. Inkster?"

"The interest of a friend, sir, of one who wishes her well."

"Nothing more?"

"I beg your pardon?"

"Nothing more than a minister's concern for the spiritual welfare of one of his flock?"

"You have put it very well. Nothing more than that. What else could there be?"

"Oh, come, come, Mr. Inkster. You have not spent your entire life up to this point holed up in the back of beyond. And even there, even there . . . well, how shall I put it . . . ?"

Now I understood what he was implying and the blood rushed to my face. I felt anger, terrible anger, and also shame, for although I might have felt hurt that Isobel did not see me as a man like other men, that was a hurt born of vanity, not desire. At that moment I realized I had not seen her, in spite of our intimate conversations, as a woman, or as a woman who had the potential to be a wife—my wife.

I think now that had I been a married man at the time I went out to the Bay, I would not have listened to the intimate details of Isobel's life in quite the same way, nor been so astonished at Mr. Morton's insinuations. I was an innocent; I knew nothing of women then. It was almost as though I was listening to a tale told by an exotic stranger. I do not mean I failed to listen carefully, intensely, but I listened, perhaps, the way we Orkney boys listened to the stories of those who had returned from the regions of ice. She might as well have been an Eskimo describing the customs of a country I had heard about but never seen.

"Your suggestion is monstrous, sir!"

Here, the doctor, who had been sitting in the corner during our interview, began to clap his hands. "Oh, call him out, Mr. Inkster. Call him out and we shall have a duel. That would give us some excitement. If no duelling pistols can be found, why, we can use Company guns. Perhaps the armourer can cut the barrels down, the way the Plains Indians do so that they can more easily shoot the buffalo while on horseback. Oh, call him out!"

Mr. Morton turned on him, furious. "Hold your tongue, you drunken fool."

"Hold yours," the doctor muttered, taking another swallow of spirits.

"I will not call you out, Mr. Morton, but I find your remarks extremely offensive."

"Why, pray? She is a woman, you are a man. Indeed, she is your countrywoman and your protegée. What more natural than that you should have designs upon her?"

"'Designs'!" My voice shook, I was so angry.

His voice was cool. "Don't get in my way, sir. If you cannot see fit to work for my plan, I strongly advise you not to work against it."

That night I thought about Isobel Gunn as a wife. I did not love her, but I felt an immense pity for her, as well as admiration for the way she had dealt with her misfortune. Her love for her son was genuine, and whatever feelings she had about his father I had seen no sign of bitterness towards

the boy whose birth had destroyed her disguise. If we lived
here at Albany, if I renewed my contract once it was up, if I
gave over all thoughts of a life with a woman as educated as
myself, a companion with whom I could discuss more than
the price of bread or bere-meal . . . But no, Mr. Morton
would never allow us to remain at Albany; we would have to
go home.

She was a good woman—would my parishioners accept
her as such? Would I be refused a living because I had married a woman with a bastard son? I had heard enough of conversations between my father and the doctor to know that
my father, at least, was not very hard on those who indulged
in carnal knowledge outside marriage. "Rebuke, exhort,
absolve," I had heard him say. The Mrs. Cloustons of the
world would cut her, but who cared about them? And James
would win hearts, how could he not?

I said nothing the next day, or the next, but by the week's
end I was determined to ask Isobel to be my wife.

On Saturday afternoon I went to the plantation in search
of her. She was in the large tipi she shared with the woman
we called Mary and Mary's family. The men had gone trapping and the women were making moccasins. Mr. Morton
might denigrate the Native women, but in many ways our
lives at the fort depended on them. They made the hundreds
of pairs of moccasins we went through each year, they made
the leather sinews for the snowshoes, they dressed the skins
of deer and moose, they were excellent navigators of the
various rivers, they acted as interpreters on many occasions.
Mary occupied a senior place among the women of the

Home Guard, and I think she approved of me because I was kind to Isobel.

"I WOULD LIKE TO TALK to you alone," he said, standing at the entrance of the tipi, letting the cold air in. She thought he had come to take her to Mr. Morton and shook her head, biting off a thread as she did so.

"It's important," he said. He turned to Mary, who was still standing, watching him. "It's important."

The chatter of the other women had ceased. Even the children, who had been tumbling about, stopped playing and were quiet. The officers of the forts did not come to the women—or not in daylight—the women went to them. They were not afraid—it was only the schoolmaster—but they were curious. But La Picotte, as they called her, the scarred woman, she was afraid; they could see it in the way she held her body, the way she called to the boy to come by her, the way she held on to him when he tried to run away.

Mary was the only one who knew why Isobel was afraid. She nodded at Isobel, and motioned for her to go out and leave the boy, spoke something to her in Cree.

He waited for her a little ways away, towards the bank of the frozen river, down a path that had been cut through the snow. The sky was a clear, merciless blue and the sun, although it cast blue shadows, gave no warmth. It was not a day to be outside unless one was moving. As soon as she appeared, as bundled and muffled as he, they began to walk.

"I would rather be in the schoolroom when we had this

conversation," he said. "It is difficult to walk and talk at the same
time. But I did not want to be overheard." He stopped, turned, and
they were nearly face to face. All he could see were her eyes.

"I know how much you love James and how you do not wish to
be parted from him."

"Nivver!" she shouted, throwing off her scarf. "Nivver, nivver,
nivver!"

"I heard you," he said. "Wrap your face up or you will freeze." He
began again: "I have thought a great deal about your dilemma . . .
but come, let us keep walking. Ach, it's too cold to carry on this conversation!" Then, to himself, But we must, I must.

Wheeled again, nearly knocking her over. "Would you consider . . ."
the words coming out too cold, each with its cloud of cold air. "Would
you consider marrying me?" Unwound his scarf completely, in case
she hadn't understood. "I would like to marry you, Isobel Gunn.
Marry you and look after your boy."

They stood facing each other for a few moments. Then she turned
and ran back the way they had come.

"Think about it," he called after her. "Think about it!" Not
knowing he had echoed Mr. Morton's very words.

She did not stop.

At dinner the doctor said, "Did I see you down by the river this
afternoon, Mr. Inkster, with one of the Native women? Should we
prepare for a country wedding?"

"Ah," said Mr. Morton, "have you fallen, Schoolmaster? I'm surprised; I thought you were made of sterner stuff."

The doctor knew, Magnus was sure of it. But Mr. Morton? He
thought not. Magnus could think of no reply, and so he remained
silent.

"Ah, leave him alone," said the doctor. "I remember those early days of love, the desire to keep the affair secret, just the two of you in the world. Lovely feeling, that is. When you know so little about one another and the whole world shimmers and dances in her presence. I wasn't always an old bachelor, you know."

"You're not an old bachelor now," said Mr. Morton. "I seem to recall a wife and a great gaggle of children back in Ireland."

"Yes, I try hard to forget. You are cruel, sir, to remind me." He sighed. "Now I shall have to get well and truly drunk."

THE NEXT DAY WAS SUNDAY. Isobel did not appear at Divine Service, and I had too much pride to try to find her after dinner. I went back to the schoolroom, muttering something about being behind in my journal. Harriet MacNeil and her brothers were the brightest of the lot, but MacNeil was also a trapper and he often took the children away with him for several days. It was hard to evaluate progress when lessons were so frequently interrupted.

It did not take me long to make up the journal, and afterwards I simply sat in the cold, darkening room, wondering why Isobel had run away from me. She could not possibly fear me, knew I had only her best interests at heart and was very much against her being torn from her child. I was not unattractive, so it couldn't be that I repelled her in that way, could it? Some of my classmates at St. Andrews had teased me because their sisters had asked when I would be visiting again. I was no longer clean-shaven, but had grown a beard;

that made me no different from the majority of the men at the fort. I couldn't believe that she preferred the almost hairless bodies of the Native men.

Perhaps I should have shaved my beard off before I approached her? I was about to go to my room and examine my face in the wavery mirror when she came silently in at the door. James was not with her.

"I'm sorry I ran," she said. "Can you light a candle?"

I did so and then we sat side by side on one of the forms, silent, awkward, watching our shadows on the walls.

"I canna stay long," she said, "but I want to thank you for your offer."

"You will consider it?"

"No."

"Nivver, nivver?" I said, teasing her a little.

"Nivver."

"Can you tell me why?"

"You'd not get a living in Orkney if you returned with such a wife and her bastard child."

"Perhaps not, but there are other things I could do. Teach in a parish school—I'm finding I like teaching—or become a writer in an office, if the synod won't have me. And maybe we wouldn't have to go home again; we could stay here at the Bay. Not at Albany Fort, but there are other places that will require schoolmasters."

"You dinna understand," she said. "He wants me gone. Clear away. And there is somethin' else."

A long silence. She reached over and scraped a bit of warm wax from the candle, rolled it into a little ball, rubbed it between her fingers. When she spoke again she turned her head, a habit she had, so that her damaged cheek was away from me.

"I must tell you I never want to be touched by a man again."

"Not all men," I said, "are like John Scarth."

"Mebbe not; I dinna wish to find out. And I maun do what's best for the boy."

"The boy would have as good an education with me as he is likely to get with Mr. Morton."

She stood up and reached out her hand. I clasped it in mine, cold hand to cold hand.

"You are sorry for me," she said. "I dinna want that. And I dinna want to marry."

"Not even to remain together with James? And we wouldn't have to marry, we could be like brother and sister; I would be happy to be uncle, if not father, to James."

She disengaged her hand.

"Goodnight, Mr. Inkster."

"I shall accompany you to the plantation."

"No. The moon is up; I can see my way clearly. And—'tis best Mr. Morton or the others not see us together. I want to come to school."

"As you wish."

Within the month she had accepted Mr. Morton's offer to bring James up as his son.

SHE THOUGHT OF JAMES growing up in a fine house, becoming educated, a gentleman with nice clothes and plenty to eat. Would he thank her, later on, for giving him this chance? Would he seek her out once he was a man, and bless her for her sacrifice? She imagined him walking up the narrow streets of Stromness, all the old gossips standing in their doorways, "Who is this fine chiel?" And he, enquiring for Mrs. Isobel Gunn, his mother. Stops at her door, looks down at her (for he would be a grand height). "Mither? 'Tis your son, James." And he would kiss her hands and she wouldna speak for weepin'.

Was that what she should do? Let him go with that cold and fussy man, Mr. Morton?

Or should they run away? She could take James and disappear until the ship came in. She could hunt and trap, keep out of sight until August, then throw herself on the mercy of Captain Hanwell. No. Not run away, for he would send some of the Home Guard after her. Not run away, pretend to agree, then, when Captain Hanwell made his visit to the fort, beg him to protect her and her son. Would he do it? She would ask Magnus.

"No," he said. "He is a Company man, after all. However kindly he felt towards your predicament, I can't see him interfering in any way."

"Then what shall I do?"

"Marry me. My offer still stands. We'll go home together."

"I canna do that."

"I don't understand you, Isobel. You want to keep the child and I offer you a way to do so. I am not a monster; I have only your welfare at heart, yours and the boy's."

"I canna."

"Can you tell me why?"

She shook her head, not sure herself what the reason was. Perhaps she was mad to refuse this good man who said he would look after her and James.

He did not understand her, and he said so. She did not understand herself, except to know their marriage would be disastrous. She did not want to be touched. He said he would respect that, but he was a man, wasn't he? Sooner or later he would want that and she couldn't bear it. There was something violent in her——she knew it. Something handed on from Father, from Mother. If he touched her, she would not be able to stop herself; she would kill him. She was good with a knife now, very good. She would have killed John Scarth if he had not been sent away to Moose Factory. Killed him herself. Come up behind him and stuck the knife in, stood there and watched him die.

She hadn't told Magnus that there was more than once, that Scarth had used her brutally and she hated him for it, was glad he had drowned. She would have loved to have seen him whirled away, beyond help. Would have laughed until her sides hurt.

In the end she went to Mr. Morton and agreed to give up the child.

BECAUSE MOST OF THE FURS had gone down to Moose Factory before I arrived, I had no idea, until the following year, what a business it was to get the cargo ready for the ship's arrival in late August. The work really began in June, as more and more canoes arrived laden with beaver from the inland posts and the various brigades unloaded their furs.

The skins were dried and stretched and then flattened under a great press in order to make compact bundles of about eighty pounds in weight. They were then wrapped in parchment to make them watertight. If a canoe should tip over, they would float.

For the summer months the world of the forts revolved around beaver, whether *castor gras*, or "greasy beaver," or *castor sec,* parchment beaver. Both kinds were in demand by the hatters of London. Every scrap was accounted for; if we wished beaver, for mitts or anything else, we had to buy it. And whatever was purchased by the Indians was purchased in "Beaver" or "Made Beaver," as though beaver was a coin and not a skin. A trade gun might "sell" for ten Made Beaver, a three-point blanket for four and so on down the list. The prices were set in London, but the doctor told me many of the traders set a higher price once the goods had arrived, then pocketed the difference.

The Natives, especially the "captains" of the brigades, expected presents as well; jackets with brass buttons, rolls of tobacco, rum, beads and handkerchiefs for their women. McTavish and MacNeil handled most of the trading, but Mr. Morton, who seemed to be respected by the Natives, would often appear, just to make sure that all was going according to plan. If the captain was very important, he might even be invited to smoke a pipe or partake of a dram in the officers' mess. Our chief did not like this part of his duty, but he knew it was important to keep up the traditional ceremonies. The Natives, except when inebriated, were very formal people.

The doctor told me that Mr. Morton had special soap,

from France, that he used to wash his hands after a bout of handshaking and ceremony, and that the cups used by the captains were later boiled. I did not see this myself, but he was always relieved when the majority of the furs were in the storeroom and most of the canoes had left. He did tell me that he did not enjoy the Christmas tradition of shaking hands with every member of our Home Guard, but only because he found it "tedious." At some forts the country wives were kissed during the Christmas reception, but this he absolutely refused to do, making the doctor stand in for him, which he did most willingly and with a great deal of banter.

"You must not mind our chief," he called to the women. "He is a bachelor, and bashful."

THE CHIEF'S LOOK OF SMUG triumph whenever he saw me was almost unendurable. I had never before felt such an overwhelming desire to smash my fist in a man's face. Isobel had not told him of my proposal and yet somehow he knew; perhaps he had planted spies outside the schoolroom door; perhaps she had told Mary and one of the Home Guard had overheard.

Mr. Morton himself came more and more to the schoolroom to examine the scholars in their alphabets and numbers and to request writing exercises to be sent to London, "For the Company ship will be here before we know it."

IN LATE AUGUST THE SLOOP arrived. It was usual, when the year's supply of goods and letters arrived at the fort, for the men to hurry with the unloading and the air to be full of laughter and good cheer. Not this time. There was none of that excitement and expectation. All went about their tasks with long faces. It was not that Isobel Gunn was such a favourite, but that the men knew in their hearts that the chief had somehow tricked her into this arrangement. Why else would a mother abandon such a child as James?

I said my farewells to her and promised to do my best for the boy until he went to England. "I'll write," I said, "and you must try to write to me as well."

As the sloop disappeared around the bend, James's frantic cries for his mother escalated into screams. In spite of Mary's gentle crooning, he would not be comforted. Mr. Morton, almost as red in the face as the child, looked helplessly at the surgeon while the Native women stood, with their children, silent and solemn and our men muttered behind him.

"Isn't there something . . . ?" Mr. Morton asked.

"It's not too late to send him after her," the surgeon said.

"No, no. The matter is settled. But there must be a way to—ah—quiet him. Until the shock wears off."

The surgeon laughed. "And when will that be, pray? He's yours now, sir; you're his parent. You think of something." With this he turned on his heel and limped back towards the fort.

Mr. Morton went over to the child, pulling out his watch and swinging it back and forth. "See, James, here's my watch. You like that, eh?"

The boy batted the watch away, screaming even louder, kicking his legs and attempting to get down and run after the boat.

Mr. Morton gave up for the time being. "Take him away," he said to Mary. "Use some of your hocus-pocus on him and bring him to me later."

She looked at him with such contempt that he quickly stepped back a pace or two, murmuring, "It's all for the best" and "She agreed to it; there was no coercion." He gave me a miserable glance as he too retreated back to the safety of the fort.

I spoke to Mary. "Will he be all right?"

She nodded.

"This should never have happened."

She nodded again.

Isobel said that she heard his screams in her nightmares for the rest of her life.

That evening I excused myself from supper and went for a long walk by the river, but the sounds of the rushing water could not soothe me. I scarcely felt the mosquitoes and other irritating winged creatures. The enormous setting sun, red and swollen, seemed to reflect my anger at the whole situation. I was furious with Morton for devising this plan and equally furious with Isobel for agreeing to it. How could she, of all people, who had lost her own mother at an early age, turn her back on the child for whom she had such obvious and deep affection? She wanted him to have a better life? The best life, surely, is to be with people who love you, rich or poor. Mr. Morton did not love James; he wanted a son, a pure white son. He despised the Natives and would no more dream of intimacy with a Native woman than he would think of deliberately exposing himself to some fatal disease. And perhaps, too, James was to be some sort of trophy for him, the way those who have been to exotic lands return with the foot of an elephant or the head of a gazelle. He would return with the first white child born in Rupert's Land. I may be wrong about this last, for he intended to formally adopt the boy and give him his name, but I had a feeling the story of James's birth and "rescue" would come out almost as soon as Mr. Morton was back in London. I suspected that he would never marry, that a housekeeper, a governess and then a tutor would be all the "family" James would ever know—Papa away at Fenchurch Street all day long. Maybe Mr. Morton's mother was a sympathetic soul—after all, she had let heart rule head and had married a Scot!

I never knew my grandparents, but I had always imagined grandmothers, at least, to be creatures of infinite patience and love. I had seen the Native grandmothers here and admired the way they combined love with discipline. At the moment, the only consolation in the whole sad affair was that James had Mary and his Indian family and playmates.

A great deal of anger was also meted out to myself. Why had Isobel refused to marry me? Why had Morton been so much more persuasive than I? She seemed shocked that I would even suggest such a thing as marriage.

Did she think she had no right to the child? Was that it? Surely not—surely she had more spirit than that?

The sun burst and stained the evening sky with red. I had walked a long way and had to turn back; soon it would be dark. Mother and son would endure their first night apart since the child's birth. James had Mary to comfort him; who would comfort Isobel?

O WE PORE MOTHERS!

Mr. Morton set out to wean James from his Indian companions, all but Mary, for he needed her. He had had a small chamber built off his apartment when Isobel first returned from Pembinah and this he made into a nursery for the child. Mary slept on a pallet near his bed. Every evening Mr. Morton spent an hour or two with the boy, talking to him, teaching him his prayers, correcting his speech, for as James grew older and his vocabulary increased, he tended to speak English in the sing-song accents of his nurse.

Another woman was now in charge of my scholars, but I requested that James be allowed to continue coming to the schoolroom, so that he could get the benefit of some early education, if only by osmosis. Morton knew that I disliked him and disapproved of what he had done; he was hesitant to let me exert any influence on James at all. Yet, like Mary, he needed me. He made me agree never to mention Isobel or in any way remind the boy of his mother. I said I thought that was monstrous.

"No, sir, it is not. Ask the surgeon. A clean cut, with a sharp knife, is better than a slow sawing away."

"We are not talking of amputation, Mr. Morton. We are talking about a heartsick child."

"The sooner he forgets about his mother, the better."

"And what are you going to tell him when he asks?"

He stared at me with his hard eyes. "I shall tell him she is dead."

"There are those who will tell him differently."

"Anyone who tells him differently will be dismissed."

"And Mary?"

"For the present, I can't do much about Mary. However, her family is very well situated here. It would be a pity if they found they could not remain as part of the Home Guard. It is a privilege, after all, not a right."

"You disgust me," I said, and got up from the table.

"Don't forget, Mr. Inkster," he called after me, "you, too, can be dismissed."

I had promised Isobel I would stay with the child; in future I would have to be more careful.

I had received a letter with the incoming packet but had put it aside, preferring to read it after Isobel's departure. Now I took it out and was surprised I hadn't noticed, in my agitation, that it was from the doctor and not my father. The letter said that my father was dead. "He keeled over, Magnus, like a great tree falling, a look of surprise upon his face—for I was with him at the time. We had just come back from a grand day tramping about the hills on Hoy. I want to assure you that he didn't suffer, and to tell you that his Norse blood thrilled to think of you in a new land across the seas. That is not to say he didn't miss you, every day, and look forward to your return—the possibility of marriage and grandchildren and the merry times we would have. There was a grand funeral, the laird present, of course, but the crowds of poor folk would have delighted him more. Now he rests next to your mother, his work here done."

He did not add what I was to discover later: that his own wife was poorly. Soon she, too, was in the ground. He had asked the laird to keep open the living and appoint a temporary minister until I had fulfilled my contract at the Bay. "He said neither yes nor no, but I believe he will consider it. Your father was a great favourite of his."

THOSE YEARS, FROM THE departure of Isobel until I too left Albany Fort, remain in my mind as something not quite real, a landscape covered in mist, the way Orkney can look, sometimes, when the haar comes rolling in from the sea. The death of my father affected me deeply; I could not accept that I would never see him again, and I was also distressed by the departure of Isobel Gunn. Mr. Morton informed me that a letter to "Jno. Fubbister" had turned up, sent to Eastmain by mistake, but there was nothing he could do about it now; he would send it on to Isobel Gunn next year.

"Have you read it?" I asked him.

"Certainly not! I may, from time to time, have to check the outgoing post, but I have never opened a sealed letter unless addressed to me."

I became more and more solitary and found it difficult to endure mealtimes with Mr. Morton and the others. I often retired to my apartment immediately after supper and read until my head ached and the words danced upon the page. Shakespeare, Dante, Bunyan, Calvin, the Bible. My annual supply of candles was becoming dangerously low. You would think that such reading would reconcile me to my situation, or at least bring me to a point where I would say— and mean it—"'Tis God's will," or "There's Divinity that shapes our ends, Rough-hew them how we will," but that was not the case. That winter was a hard one. Many of the Natives had coughs, as did some of the men. I, too, developed a cough, my old childhood companion. The surgeon was kept busy with his balsamic mixtures, his salves and camphorated oil.

My solace was the schoolroom, where the children came and went according to their fathers' occupations, but were all happy to apply themselves when present. James and Mary came for a half-hour at the end of lessons, and by the time of his second birthday he knew his alphabets and could even arrange his wooden letters (much worn now and exhibiting teeth marks) into simple words. But he was never the same merry child after Isobel left; in fact, he had grown quite thin and looked out at the world in a solemn manner that broke my heart. In the New Year he came down with a severe attack of hooping cough. Many on the plantation had succumbed to this scourge, and some of the servants were ill as well. There were four days when the entire fort was hushed and anxious as the surgeon, sober for once, struggled to save him. He recovered, but now he was thinner than ever and so listless we wondered if his brain had been affected by the fever.

Mary requested that she take him back to her family for a while. Morton refused, but when it became clear to him that the child's recovery was ominously slow, he finally agreed. A dead child was no use to him and, in fact, could cause a scandal that might wreck his career.

So Mary and James moved out of the small nursery for a few weeks and went back to live on the plantation. I have no idea how she managed it—spells or medicines or simply a different environment (with happy memories of his mother, perhaps)—but from that time on he began to pick up, much to everyone's relief, and although he and Mary were forced to move back within the fort, there was no relapse.

James often sat with the old carpenter or the tailor, both of whom gave him scraps to play with. The tailor had been instructed to make him some "proper" clothing, but since what he wore was not that different from what the Natives wore—at least in winter—he soon got used to his new breeches and shirts. As his feet grew, Mary kept him supplied with moccasins for within and without.

Mr. Morton took him for rides in his cariole on occasion, but he would not go unless Mary or I accompanied him in another. The chief factor pretended that nothing was wrong, that of course he wanted one of us to go along, but it was easy to see that he did not take this rejection lightly. He began to talk to James of London and all the wonderful things they would do there, and of how they would visit the uncle's country estate. Perhaps James would like a pony of his very own? Since all of this was going to take place in some nebulous future, James treated it as a story and dismissed it.

In the springtime I took him for walks along the river, his small hand in mine. Once we saw a cow moose and her calf, once a mother bear and her cub, fishing together on the opposite bank. I began to teach him the names of trees and flowers, only to discover that he knew them all—in Cree.

In early summer, we searched for wild strawberries and raspberries, which the cook made into jam. The air was a spicy mix of balsam and juniper and wild roses. This was the loveliest time at the bottom of the Bay, and it made one forget the long winter that had preceded it and the hot summer, with its legions of stinging insects, that was to come. James regained his weight and colour, if not his merry smile.

The Berdash appeared one day in the midst of a group of inland Natives who had arrived with a load of furs. Mary told me he asked after Isobel and shook his head angrily when informed she had been sent away. If he let Mary know what he had seen, she never told. Mr. Morton refused him entrance into the hall, saying he was a corrupting influence on the men. The Berdash shouted something in reply, lifted his skirts and did a little obscene, capering dance until all the men were laughing. Mr. Morton, in retaliation, denied the Natives any credit—or any rum—for three days. This seemed a risky business, but they capitulated; a formal apology was offered by the captain, a pipe was smoked and things went back to normal. What a temptation it must have been for that strange creature, so reviled by this white man, to state the truth about one of the chief factor's men: that he raped Isobel Gunn, and that the little boy he coveted so was the result of this rape. Did he keep silent, even when grotesquely drunk, because Isobel had kept silent or because he feared he would not be believed?

James never mentioned his mother; had Mary told him not to? Mr. Morton was attempting to teach him to address him as Father, but he clamped his lips shut and shook his head.

"Very well. I can see that I'm rushing things. That will come in time."

In the middle of my third winter, Mr. Morton, on one of his sketching expeditions, stumbled into a trap and badly gashed his leg. It was fortunate that one of the Home Guard, returning through the forest, heard his cries for help or he might have died from the cold. As it was, he needed many stitches and, in spite of the doctor's unguents, the wound turned septic. He had to conduct the business of the fort from his office, with his leg up on a cushioned chair, and it was not until springtime that he was able to move about freely—and even then only with the help of a cane.

During this time he was very morose at meals and some evenings equalled, or even surpassed, the doctor in his tip-pling. Nevertheless, he spent a half-hour with James each evening, quizzing him on his activities. Then Mary took the lad away to bed. I went along to hear his bonie-words, and then I too retired to my apartment to read.

One afternoon I was tutoring James in the schoolroom. I can't remember now exactly what we were doing, but I think it was numbers—he was very quick with numbers, and if anyone asked him how old he was he would reply, very seriously, "Three years and four munts," without resort to his fingers. I think we had a pile of nails we were using for counters, one long nail equalling ten of the smaller sort. We were both sitting on the dusty floor because it was easier that way. He laughed and clapped his hands when he discovered that two groups of five nails was the same as a group of three and seven, which was the same as a group of ten all in a row.

"You are a very clever boy," I said. Delighted by his delight, I picked him up and hugged him. The feel of his arms around my neck loosed something in me, some deep pool of affection I hadn't known about, and I simply sat there with the little boy on my lap, knowing I could never desert him so long as he needed me.

"Father," he said.

If my heart were an egg, then I had, for my own self-protection, built up such a hard shell around it that no chick of sentiment would ever be able to peck its way out. But this chick had done the right thing; with that one word he had pierced the shell from the outside and made his way in.

Why that word? Perhaps some old, forgotten memory of flinging my infant arms about my own father's neck or knees? I don't know, but from that day forward I was determined to stand by James and commit myself to his well-being.

Mr. Morton came in at just that moment.

"Hello, James," he said. "How are you getting on?" He gave a little grimace of distaste at my dusty trousers and casual position on the floor.

James looked up at him, still with his arms around my neck.

"Father," he said. But he pointed his finger at me. Then buried his face in my neck.

NO MATTER HOW I PROTESTED, Mr. Morton would not believe I had nothing to do with James's declaration. That evening he was in such a red-faced rage, I thought he would drop dead from apoplexy at any minute.

"You are trying to turn that child against me!"

"I have said not one word against you, sir, not one."

"Oh, you're a subtle one, Schoolmaster. I'm sure you have your wordless ways. I put you in a position of the highest trust, the *highest* trust, as regards that boy, and this is how you repay me. You and his nurse—you probably cooked this up together."

He was so angry the spit flew out of his mouth.

"No, sir, we did not."

"Then why did he call you Father—unless you taught him to do so?"

"I don't know. I think it was just a spontaneous thing. He likes numbers and he had just discovered something. I had helped him to that discovery. 'Father,' in that sense."

"What sense?"

"Guide, helper, person in authority—I don't know. I was as startled as you were."

"I have been trying to get him to call me Father."

"Yes, I know."

"He refuses. He gives me black looks. Why is that, Mr. Inkster?"

"I don't know. Somehow he must associate you with his mother's absence. Even a small child would understand that you are in control of this fort and everyone in it."

"Does he talk about his mother? Does he accuse me of anything?"

"No—to both questions. He never mentions her, and I have never heard him say ill of you."

He sat down heavily, but did not motion me to sit. "It's that witch, Mary; she has set him against me."

"I don't think so, sir. I think she is a very loyal servant."

"You don't know what she tells him when they are alone."

"I know she wishes to do nothing to distress him, sir."

"Then why—*why*—does he call you Father and not me? It makes no sense."

"Little children don't always make sense—and that was the first and only time."

"You would swear to that?"

"I swear it."

"You did not coach him?"

"No, sir."

"Very well, you may go."

I left with a sense of foreboding. Oh, James! The very word that had pierced my heart and made me love you as a father was to be our undoing, I knew it.

Another woman, Ellen, country wife of McTavish, now accompanied Mary and the boy wherever they went and was obviously employed to spy on them. Only at night, in their closet, were they left alone. And although I continued to teach him, we went for no more walks together unless Ellen was with us. I decided to try and ignore her, to be as open and friendly with James as I could be, to swing him in the air, to hug him, laugh with him, let him know he had a masculine friend and protector. I took Mary aside and explained what had happened in my interview with Mr. Morton. I told her to convey to James that he must never call me Father again, that I loved him as a father, but that Mr. Morton was to be his legal father, could he not try to call Mr. Morton thus? I had no idea how she would explain this to such a young child, but I left it to her.

I told James and the other children—if they had done well—stories of the gods and giants of Norse legend, as well as stories from Aesop's fables and *The Pilgrim's Progress*. When I talked of Sleipnir, the six-legged horse of Odin, I wished I had such a magic beast to carry me and James away home to Orkney.

IN JULY 1811, MR. MORTON called me in and dismissed me. Even though I had feared this would happen, I fought it.

"May I ask on what grounds?"

"Unsuitability, Mr. Inkster."

"In what way am I unsuitable, sir? I had thought you were pleased with the way my scholars had progressed."

He leaned back in his chair, tipping it back so far that I

was sure it would fall at any moment. "Oh, I daresay you are competent enough. I didn't say you were incompetent; I said you were unsuitable." He paused, tipped the chair forward again. "It's your attitude, Mr. Inkster; you are arrogant and insolent and"—another pause—"you have strayed from what you were hired to teach. You tell these impressionable children pagan tales. If that is not unsuitability, tell me what is."

I had made it clear to the children that the Norse stories were pagan ("only stories"), but I refused to argue the point. I had something far more weighty to discuss.

"If you are dismissing me, sir, let me take the boy with me."

He said nothing. The awful icy silence went on and on. The surgeon was performing an amputation, and as all the doors were open, I could hear the man's screams from far away in the east flanker.

"She gave the boy to me, sir, not to you. She wishes him raised as a gentleman." Hands shaking, he opened a drawer, then thrust a piece of paper at me. "See, see? Her name is affixed to this document; it is all legal and binding."

There, in a shaky but legible hand, I could see her signature: *Isobel Gun.* And it was I who had taught her to write her name.

THE NIGHT BEFORE I LEFT Albany Fort, I spent an uncomfortable evening with Mr. Morton, the doctor and the two traders. Mr. Morton had searched my kist before I locked it.

I had been given several small wrapped parcels by my fellow countrymen, to deliver to their loved ones, and he insisted upon opening them all.

"Routine, Mr. Inkster, when men are returning home."

Knowing the officers' baggage was never examined, I wanted to get up on my high horse and say, "I am not exactly one of the men, sir," but I held my tongue. Did he think there was anything I wished to steal except James?

I cleared my throat after supper. "When do you intend to take James to London, Mr. Morton?"

"Why do you wish to know? Do you plan to pay us a visit there?"

"No, sir, my future plans do not include England."

"Well, I will tell you just the same. In two years my incarceration here will be over. At that time, we shall return home and live with my mother in London."

"And Mary? What will become of her?"

He attempted a puzzled look. "Why, what should become of her? She will remain here. She would hardly get on in Mayfair, Mr. Inkster!"

I nodded. "I agree, but she is James's foster mother, and the ties between them are strong. I fear he will go into a decline when those ties are severed so abruptly."

"Nonsense. He has survived his mother's departure; he will easily survive a break with his nurse. And he will have all London to explore. He will have proper books and a good tutor. A pony perhaps. Suitable companions of his own age. Mary and his life here will cease to interest him. Youth is resilient, Mr. Inkster. My father died when I was a lad. I was unhappy, of course, but soon he was nothing but a memory."

"And if it had been your mother? Mary is almost as much his mother as Isobel Gunn. Mary suckled him after his mother left."

"Yes, indeed." He made a grimace of distaste. "He has had two barbarians for mothers, unfortunate boy. It puts one in mind of St. Paul: 'Then I saw as through a glass darkly.' He has seen through a very dark glass, has he not? Soon he will greet his own world, the world where he belongs, 'face to face.'"

"It is you, sir," I muttered, "who see through a dark glass."

"I beg your pardon?"

"It was nothing."

"I hope so, Mr. Inkster. I shall assume it was nothing. Goodnight."

I WAS ALLOWED A BRIEF private goodbye with James.

"Will you see my mama?"

He startled me; I had not mentioned Isobel to him since she left. I looked in anguish to Mary, who was standing slightly apart from us. She nodded.

"Yes, I hope to see your mother. I shall tell her what a fine boy you have become."

"Tell her I can count," he said, and began, "one, two, tree, four . . ."

I turned my face away.

An hour later, he stood solemnly at the water's edge,

with Mary beside him. Mr. Morton stood behind, with a hand on each small shoulder. Some of my scholars stepped forward. Having secretly rehearsed a hymn, they sang it through, looking shyly at their feet, then one by one they gravely shook my hand. Drumming and chanting began from the plantation.

The carpenter, the armourer, the men who, if not exactly friends, had been my companions in the wilderness, said their farewells. Several patted my shoulder, whispered, "We'll keep an eye on him, buddo."

I had developed a certain admiration for the doctor, and was pleased when he, too, stepped forward, shook my hand and wished me a safe journey. Mr. Morton nodded his head, but did not move from his watchful position behind James.

It was a beautiful morning, with the mist rising over the water and the poplars beginning to turn. Soon the geese would fly south, the cold would come, the snow, the ice, and the cycle would begin again. When you know you are seeing something for the last time, how you long to capture the scene, to have the talent of a painter. There was Mr. Morton in his official uniform, his blue frock coat and top hat, his men behind him in clean smocks and white trousers. Mary had dressed herself in her finest dress and leggings, her long black hair done back in a single plait. The wooden palisade rose up behind us; I had become used to the sight and smell of wood, to dense forests and the creatures that inhabited them. I said to myself, Remember this, remember this. Remember James as he looks today.

The men began to sing as they pulled upon the oars. We were using one of the new boats, modelled on our Orkney yoles, and my fellow countrymen were highly pleased with them, never, with a few exceptions, having been comfortable with paddling, for we were not raised on it like the Canadians. Rowing was in our blood.

Over the singing, as we approached the bend in the river, I heard a single shrill cry, "Father, goodbye!" Oh, James, were you punished for that?

Did those hands, laid so possessively on your shoulders, bear down hard in fury at your betrayal? Did your new father hate you at that moment? Did you feel, through those trembling hands, that hate?

WHEN I STEPPED ON BOARD the *Prince of Wales*, Captain Hanwell acknowledged me with a friendly nod.

"Well, Mr. Inkster, I hope you will take advantage of my hospitality, as before." It was from him that I heard of Isobel's journey back to Orkney, and of her sad homecoming.

"Where is she now, do you know?"

"Indeed. She is living in Stromness and she has her sister's child with her, a little girl. Her sister died in childbirth."

"Is Isobel all right?"

"I have seen her only when the ship comes in on the homeward journey. She asks for letters about the boy."

"I have written to her; did she not receive my letters?"

"She did not. No doubt they were confiscated, either by

Mr. Morton or Mr. Geddes. We have orders not to speak to her about him."

"How cruel! I suspected Mr. Morton would not write to her, but I have been faithful to my promise. The man is a monster."

"Cruel as it may seem, Mr. Inkster, perhaps it is for the best."

"How so? She is his mother."

"She has given him up in the hope of a better life for him than what she has endured. She cannot have it both ways."

"But she should have news of him, surely? And James should know of her letters."

"Do you think it is good for a child to know his mother has given him up?"

"For good reasons? This is not a case of abandonment, Captain Hanwell."

"Explain that to the child. Isobel is a strong woman, and if she cared a fig what others think, she would not have disguised herself as a lad and run off to Rupert's Land. She could have brought the boy up; she is not a woman to give way. I was most surprised she agreed to it, for now I think she has changed her mind."

"But you yourself just said she gave him up so that he would have a better life."

"Yes, but will he? The very poor look at the well-to-do and think their life is better. Easier, certainly. And I fear Isobel Gunn is at heart a romantic. Mr. Morton has promised to make of her son a gentleman."

"'Gentleman' was the magic word he used."

He sighed. "Mr. Inkster, do you know London at all?"

"No, sir, I have never been south of the Borders. I should like to visit London one day, but I doubt it will happen."

"Well, if you knew London, I would need to say no more when I say I was born in the Devil's Half-Acre. My parents were poor and we were often hungry. But there was love in the house; love can fill the soul and help one to endure an empty stomach. I was lucky; I was sent to the Grey Coat School to learn to be a seaman. Now I am captain of a Company ship and will be until I retire. My son is following in my footsteps. I saw my parents regularly until they died and was able, in their later years, to provide comforts they had never known before. That's one thing. But a heart divided? A boy who grieves for a mother who gave him up so that he might have a full belly and fine clothes and yet clings to him in letters? Will he not be always full of anger and guilt? She made her choice. Now she must let him go."

"She made her choice in extraordinary circumstances and under duress."

"She could have said no."

"Perhaps she did not realize how hard it would be."

"Aye, the poor girl, I think that is so. But it's too late now."

I CANNOT IMAGINE THE horror of Isobel's first hours back in Orkney. She had not expected to be met, for Jannet and her new family lived in Kirkwall, but she had also not expected the stares and whispers of those gathered at the pier to have a look at her. Even the children taunted her with a rhyme:

Isobel Gunn, Isobel Gunn
Put on breeks and awa' she run.

She pushed her way through the crowd and presented herself at Mr. Geddes's office to receive her back wages. Mr. Morton, it turned out, had never reduced her salary to that of a washerwoman, so she was grateful she had more money than she expected. Leaving her sea-kist with a chandler's wife who had a back room full of things she stored for sailors, Isobel set out on the long walk to Kirkwall.

The town of Stromness frightened her. It seemed noisy and crowded and the rain and grey stone combined to drive her spirits even lower. She experienced none of that lifting of the heart the traveller usually feels when, having braved the dangers of an ocean voyage, he finds himself back on land. Wearing no bonnet, wrapped in a dark shawl, she tried to keep her head up, determined not to weep. At least she had some money; she would give it to Jannet immediately she arrived at the house.

She walked for hours and arrived, muddy, drenched, hungry, after dark. When, after making enquiries, she finally found the wee house in a lane behind the Girnell, she was so weary it took her a moment to understand the meaning of the crepe on the door. She knew it was for Jannet even before she raised a trembling hand and knocked.

The young husband, over his family's objections, gave the baby into Isobel's care. His wife's dying words had commanded him to do so "when Isobel comes home." She would have to find lodgings, however, elsewhere. It would not be seemly for her to remain with the young husband. She spent the night on a rug by the fire and kept her own sorrows to herself. She had imagined telling Jannet about James, unburdening herself to her sister—and now Jannet was gone. She did not want this other baby thrust upon her, but in the middle of the night, when she heard its cry, she got up automatically and went to it. "Husha, husha," wrapping it tight against her, falling asleep with the child in her arms.

I had written a long letter to my father, a letter that had been handed to the doctor that very day, as he had travelled to Stromness on business. Once he was back home and the letter read, he made all haste to seek out Isobel and find lodgings for her with a widow and her spinster daughter. But, she told me later, they were respectable people and she was no longer used to the company of women. They found her uncouth and quarrelsome. After two months she took the little girl, named Nellie, and removed them both to Stromness.

YOUR CSN NELLIE IS gon to Edburg.

She became a fixture in the town, a known oddity, the "Nor-Waster," as famous as the old woman who sold fair winds to sailors. Some got it into their heads that Nellie was the love-child from the Bay. To be sure, she had the same red hair as her "auntie." Noo, noo, said others, 'tis her sister's child; she drowned t'other one, the boy.

The old women stood like crows in the doorways, knitting as they gossiped, *caw, caw, caw*; Isobel did not deign to turn her head. Nellie came home from her first day at the parish school and declared she would never go back. Isobel took her by the hand and led her there every morning for three months, until Nellie too learned to ignore the taunts of the other children: her auntie was her mother; her auntie was a witch; her auntie was fair daft, dressin' up as a man. Nellie concentrated on her alphabets. "Bugger you," she said, but only inside her head, as her auntie had taught her. "Bugger you. Go to hell."

Mr. Walter Scott came to see this extraordinary woman when he was on his tour. She wouldn't let him in.

"I didna want to be some daft creetur in one of his books."

When she and Nellie negotiated with the sailors for the sale of knitted stockings, she let her niece do the talking. They were always together, except when Nellie was at school. For several years they managed very well—enough to eat, a place to sleep, oil for the cruisie, peats for the fire. Each was lonely in her own fashion, but together they faced the world. When my old friend the doctor called, Isobel was polite but firm: they were fine; they did not need help. Except for her reputation, she could have been any of dozens of women whose men were dead or away in the New World. Except that she had been there; she was the only one who had actually been there. At night, as they sat knitting before the fire, she told Nellie what it had been like in the months she was John Fubbister. She laughed and her eyes shone. But if ever she mentioned Mary or her child, then her tears fell on the wool in her lap and she could not go on.

"Nivver mind, Auntie," the child said. "You have me."

WHEN I ARRIVED AT STROMNESS, the doctor was there to meet me with his horse and cart. We immediately set off for Orphir, as I could not rest until I had visited my father's grave.

"Such a turn-out for the funeral, Magnus. Your father was a man well-loved. And now he rests beside your dear mother."

"Do you believe they have been reunited in heaven, Doctor?"

He frowned. "I believe we have a soul."

"And does one soul recognize another after death?"

"I would like to think yes."

"So my father's soul would recognize my mother's?"

"Yes."

The stone had been chosen at the time of my mother's death, and the weather had dulled the chiselled name of my father so that it looked as though it, too, had been there for a long time. It was peaceful in the churchyard, sheep grazing among the stones, but I did not feel at peace.

"I am a hypocrite, Doctor; I go about as a man of the cloth and yet I cannot believe in such reunions after death. Will my mother's soul have aged along with my father's body here on earth? Do the souls of infants remain infants, or do they too grow and mature?"

"I don't think reason will get you very far when it comes to questions of the soul and of life beyond the grave."

"Did my father believe in this poppycock?"

"Your father believed most sincerely that somehow he and Morag would be reunited."

"And predestination?"

"Ah, that I'm not sure about. We tended to avoid the subject of the elect and the damned."

He laid his hand on my arm.

"What your father had, more than anyone else I've ever known, was a belief in the healing power of love. But he approached this in a very practical way. Love had to be demonstrated through charity and good deeds. It was not enough to love your neighbour in any abstract way—you must help your neighbour, most particularly your poorer neighbour: beremeal as well as blessings." He paused. "Your father was very proud of you; he sensed a little of your hesitation, shall we call it, on certain articles of faith. But it did not make him any less convinced that you had chosen the right calling.

"Predestination," said the doctor, after a silence. "Is this not just another way to look at fate?"

"But we are talking about eternity, Doctor, not why some man prospers and another falters here below! We are talking about the saved and the damned."

"Nevertheless, we are a superstitious people, you know that yourself. We call wrecked ships godsends, even when we know a misplaced lantern or two may have helped the catastrophe along. We may help things along, but still we believe in fate.

"We believe that spirits are all around us, both good and ill. Is it such a great leap to think that eternity will not be much different? Some will be saved; some lost, or damned. This would not seem unreasonable to one whose life is ruled by fate."

"My life is not ruled by fate; I make my own fate."

The doctor sighed and shook his head. "I hope none of the trows are listening at this moment."

"So the good man may still go to hell?"

"Strictly speaking, yes. Or the good woman. But Our Lord blessed the Magdalene and prized chattering Mary over her serious sister in the kitchen. Our Lord saw goodness in strange places, and I think that gives us a clue about the saved and the damned."

With that, he suggested we turn around, for the wind had come up and a storm was brewing.

"Home," he said, "perhaps there will be jam with our bannocks for tea. My daughter and the good wives still supply me with jam, and thanks to you, my dear, I am now rich in marmalade as well. Perhaps such pleasures will sit well upon our stomachs after a walk and a philosophical discussion."

I looked around at the landscape I loved so well.

"Mr. Morton is determined to cause trouble for me."

"Aye, I can believe that. No doubt a letter is, at this very minute, being delivered via Mr. Geddes to your patron. You know that your father's living has been granted to someone else, on the assumption that you would still be at the Bay for several years?"

I hadn't known that. I had assumed there was an interim

minister who would graciously hand over to me, if not this
Sunday, then by the next.

"What, then, am I to do?"

"Come along home now, and we'll put our thinking
caps on."

THINKING CAPS HAD NOT got us very far the night before, so
decisions about my future could wait a day or two. The next
morning I borrowed the doctor's horse and sought out Isobel
Gunn, who was living in Stromness.

When I knocked upon the door, she called out in a wary
voice, "Who's there?"

"Magnus Inkster," I said.

The door was flung open almost immediately.

"Oh, Magnus, you've brought the boy! Where is he? Oh,
let me see him!"

I shook my head. "James is still at the Bay, with Mr.
Morton."

She gave me such a look! And then said, cold as ice,
"Then why are you here?"

"I was dismissed."

"Dismissed! How could he dismiss you? You promised
me you would look after my son."

"I tried to persuade him otherwise, but he would not
listen."

"You didn't try hard enough."

"Believe me, Isobel, I did."

As she stood there in silence, staring, a wee red-headed girl peeked out from beneath her skirts.

"Is this Jannet's child?" I asked.

She stepped back into the house and shut the door in my face. No amount of entreaty would convince her to open to me again, and I was gathering a curious crowd of children and old women. I returned to the doctor's house in Kirkwall, determined to write her a letter, explain everything that had happened and beg her to let me help her. There was no reply.

DERE MR. MORTON, PLEAS.

Since no living could be found for me in Orphir or the surrounding parishes (all of a sudden there seemed as many ministers as gulls in Orkney), and since I did not wish ever again to be a tutor to a rich man's sons, I became schoolmaster, for a while, at a mortification school in Stenness. I lodged with a miller and his family, and my clothes and hair seemed always to be covered with a light dusting of snow. I had twenty-four scholars, boys and girls of mixed ages and mixed sexes, both. The work was not unpleasant; the miller's family were merry and the wife a good, plain cook. They were very interested in my tales of life at the Bay, and the two oldest boys, who were part of my complement of scholars, said they had every intention of going to the New World as soon as they could. I could see that this pained the miller and his wife, so I began to point out the hardships as well as the great distance there would be between them and the rest of the family. They declared 'twould make no difference, but the miller gave me a grateful smile.

Every week I visited my parents' grave and often spent Sundays with the doctor, my one real link with the happiness of my early childhood. Sometimes the doctor's daughter and family joined us. Isobel Gunn would have nothing to do with me, no matter how many letters I wrote, and this distressed me more than I would admit, even to myself, let alone the doctor.

Although I knew that Mr. Morton was determined to separate James from anyone in Isobel's camp, and that I had done my best to persuade him to let me stay on, I still felt as though I had let her down. The look of joy on her face when she thought I had arrived with her son told me without words how much she missed him and how bitterly she must regret her decision. I thought of trying to get back to the Bay, not with the Company, but perhaps as a settler in the new colony I had heard was forming on the Red River. If so, I must seek me a wife. There were many bonny lasses in the area, and the doctor also had a habit of inviting young ladies and their mamas to Sunday tea when I was there. I don't know what held me back; I was thirty-nine years old and lonely, tired of living as a boarder, yearning for my own hearth and home and perhaps a child or two to brighten my old age. The doctor warned me often enough.

"And why do you not marry again?" I asked him.

"I suppose I became used to a certain woman, accustomed to a certain voice, a certain step upon the stair. After

she died, well, I couldn't imagine sharing my life with
another woman. And I must admit, I had your father as companion; he was very good to me. My wife, like your own
mother, was a rare woman, not like some of these silly creatures in Kirkwall."

"Yet you invite these silly creatures and their daughters
to tea."

"The least silly, I assure you. But don't be too nice,
Magnus, or you'll end up an old bachelor warming yourself
at someone else's hearth. You are thirty-seven years old, and
a living will open up for you sometime soon. A minister's life
is a hard one; it will drain you if you take it seriously. The
support of a good woman lightens the load."

A living did become available, but in Edinburgh. The
principal of St. Mary's, with whom I had remained in contact, wrote that the minister of St. Margaret's Church had
died, very suddenly, of apoplexy, and through the influence
of Lord Pitmillie, the congregation had agreed to invite me
to take up the living.

"The church is in the middle of a very fine crescent in the
New Town," he wrote, "with a very prosperous congregation.
They were somewhat reluctant to take a minister from the
remote northern islands, for fear they might not understand
you. However, I vouched for your manners and morals, as
well as your accent. I am confident you will not let me down."

"Take it! Take it!" said the doctor, as I dithered, un-
decided.

"I had not envisaged leaving Orkney again."

"Needs must, Magnus. This sounds like an excellent

living, and I can give you letters of introduction to various medical men I know there. I visited Edinburgh quite often when I was at St. Andrews."

"It will be hard for me to leave you, sir," I said with feeling. "You have always been such a good friend to me."

"You are the son of my two dearest friends. But you are also an interesting person in your own right, an intelligent, questioning, rather solitary fellow, but I think you have within you a great capacity for love. It may well be that this will manifest itself as love for a congregation rather than love for a particular person. I hope you will experience both, but we shall see."

Before I left, we had one last walk to Orphir. It was July and I made up a posy as we went, yellow seggies and bog cotton, daisies, some wild flax with its bright blue flowers. I laid it on my parents' grave. I had no idea when I would return.

"I shall visit here," the doctor said gently. "I find this a most comforting place."

"Comforting?"

"Aye."

The next day he saw me to the harbour, where I would take a boat to Leith.

"I never thought," I said, "that I would come home only to go away again."

"I think you will like Edinburgh."

"I've never lived in a big city."

"But you have lived in the company of strangers before and you survived."

"Barely."

"Oh, come, come. No more black thoughts. Write to me whenever you can and look up some of the names I have given you. They may have sons or daughters worth knowing."

I hesitated for one moment. "I have a request."

"What is it? If I can possibly comply, I shall."

"I would like, once established, to send a bit of money home from time to time. For Isobel Gunn."

"That could be arranged. You wish me to administer it?"

I nodded.

"I shall be happy to do so."

I wrote a letter to Isobel, telling her of my appointment in Edinburgh and saying I would send my address as soon as I was settled. If she ever needed me, she was to let me know. I even tried to call on her on my way to the harbour, but she shouted at me through the door, told me to go away. I set off for Edinburgh with a heavy heart.

ONE OF MY PARISHIONERS was a bonny woman named Margaret Laidlaw, from Galashiels, a widow whose husband had died in the Peninsular War. She had three daughters, the oldest a young lady, the youngest barely eight years old. They attended church every Sunday and Margaret smiled shyly at me after the service. Smiles turned to a few words and then whole sentences. After a year I felt we were well-enough acquainted that I could ask her if she would be my wife. However, I knew I must tell her about my spiritual doubts.

How to explain that there was no blinding light, nor even a blinding darkness, but merely a growing conviction that this life on earth was all the life there was, and that I felt it my duty not to frighten (or flatter) my congregation with talk of predestination and the fires of hell, but to comfort and console, the sort of things one usually associates with the minister's wife and not the minister. That I had accepted the living in Edinburgh because I was trained to be a minister, to *minister*, and that I wanted to be in a position where I could do some good in the world.

I worked hard on my sermons, and my congregation seemed pleased with me. They were, after all, the well-to-do and considered themselves, for the most part, safely among the elect. I think they saw heaven as another New Town, full of spaciousness, elegant squares and plenty of servants to keep the whole thing going. They were democratic in this, at any rate; some percentage of the labouring and servant classes had to be saved or there would be no one to wait on them. I could not ask Margaret to marry me without I confessed all.

"Do you no believe in God at all?" she said, her voice a whisper.

"I believe in God, yes, as a First Principle, perhaps, an Ordering Agent. But I do not believe in the kind of God who would select only certain people to enter heaven. I don't, in any case, believe in heaven."

"And Jesus Christ?"

"Oh, yes—the ultimate Good Man—the Example."

"But not the Son of God?"

"We are all the sons and daughters of God. Christ was a preacher, a very ordinary man with extraordinary qualities. I think perhaps he believed he was sent by God."

"Are you sure he wasna right?"

"Not positive, no." I took her hand. "Could you marry a man who thinks as I do and yet remains in the church?"

She looked at me with her clear brown eyes. "I'm no sure. You're a brave man to tell me all this."

"I could have no secrets from my wife."

Three days I waited and then she came to me.

"I do not think you are a man of no faith, Magnus." She paused. "I told my children their father is in heaven."

"Did you describe this heaven?"

"No. But I suspect they see it as a very Scottish heaven. They were worried that since he died in Spain, his soul might go to a Spanish-speaking heaven, but I said there would be but one language and all who went would speak it."

"Do *you* believe you will see your husband again?"

"Aye. Oh, not in his uniform, not bodily, but I will know him."

"Then your answer to me must be no."

She smiled. "My answer to you is yes."

WE DELAYED OUR WEDDING ceremony in the hopes that the doctor could join us. It became important to me to have his blessing in person. We had corresponded, in a desultory fashion, ever since I removed to Edinburgh, and I now wrote him a long letter with my news and invitation, and Margaret added a bit at the bottom. I managed to get the letter on a boat going up from Leith, so it wasn't too long before I had a reply. If we could wait until the first week in July, he would be able to make a fairly extended visit and would be delighted to stand by me at my wedding. We duly published the banns, and were married on a lovely July morning, in a simple ceremony, with only the doctor, myself, Margaret, her daughters, her mother (for her father was long dead) and the minister from the neighbouring parish of St. Stephen's present. It was my voice that trembled and my voice that shook; Margaret spoke out loud and clear.

The doctor treated us all to a wedding breakfast and in the afternoon we held open house for the congregation. The doctor supplied some single-malt whisky for the men, and the ladies of the congregation outdid themselves with offerings of cakes and scones. That night Margaret and I became truly man and wife. How could I not believe in God?

WHEN THE DOCTOR RETURNED to Orkney, he wrote me a letter; I have it still.

"Ach, Magnus, my pen shakes now with the infirmity of age. I should have written sooner, but I was so weary after the long journey north I gave myself my own advice and took to my bed with instructions to Mrs. Low that I was to be dosed regularly with whisky and hot water! Mrs. L., who has never been off this island, makes her noises like a mother hen and gives me I-told-him-this-would-happen looks and scolds my daughter for not stopping me.

"But my dear friend, I would not have missed it for the world. What a change has come over Edinburgh in the half-century since I saw it last! In spite of the hills, to call it the Athens of the North is nonsense, of course—one wants marble for that, and the honey-coloured light of the Mediterranean; one wants less clothing and more sunlight—but Mr. Craig's New Town is very grand indeed and Princes Street is a marvel. For a city to have such pleasant gardens in which to promenade, open to all (well, nearly all), is good for the health of its citizenry, encouraging walks in even the most elderly.

"As for the Old Town, that is another story, as you and your dear wife know only too well. How can one look any-where but down, in an attempt to avoid the worst of the filth in the streets? And the stench! Nothing I have seen or made complaint about at home prepared me for the foetid air of a dozen or more crowded into one room, in a tall hive of such a myriad of one-roomed cells, with no drains to carry away the waste. Add to that the cows and horses and pigs beneath the stairs! The squalor is horrifying; all the way home I kept resisting the urge to scrub myself again and again.

"What is the answer to such a terrible situation? Country people will pour into the cities, many with few skills and less education, thinking things will be brighter and better than at home. This seems particularly true of the Irish. I would say the city fathers, thinking they are safe from this in their fine dwellings 'across the valley,' should watch out that these wretched people do not rise up and murder them all. I would say this except that they seem for the most part far too lethargic, too beaten down, to start a revolution.

"The poor here are in a bad way and get little enough in way of support from parish funds, but they are nothing like the poor of Edinburgh.

"But I do not wish to end on a rant. It warmed my heart to see you in a 'safe harbour' at last, in your own parlour and surrounded by your pretty family. I think it charming that the bonnet was the first thing you noticed about Margaret, the way it was always just a wee bit askew as she walked into church with her little brood behind her. I suspect she is a woman completely devoid of vanity and was so busy making sure her girls were decent she never gave herself so much as a glance in the mirror! They are a credit to her, those girls; friendly without being coy or flirtatious, and so very obviously proud of and devoted to their new father. I wish you all the joy in the world and am sad only that your mother and father cannot know of it. But perhaps they do; you and I, the doubting Thomases, might be wrong, you know. Does Margaret know of your doubts? Of course she does.

"By the way, upon my return I made my usual enquiries about Isobel Gunn. She had moved house while I was gone, and is now sharing a dwelling near Brinkie's Brae, quite near the harbour, with two other women (one the relict of a man who was out at the Bay). Her niece is still with her, of course.

I do not think she is in want. Sailors will never cease needing stockings, and I've been told hers are considered as good
as those made by the women of Shetland. High praise,
indeed.

"Mrs. Low has come in and insists I lay down my pen and
lay down my head. (I have been writing this on a slope, in
bed, and now Mrs. Low, etc.).

"My best to you and Margaret and the girls,

"(P.S. Your father always said it was Morag's wild black
curls that caught his eye.)"

"CAN YOU PICTURE ME," I wrote to the doctor, "down on my
knees in the parlour, pretending to be some fantastical beast
of burden young Margaret has under her command? When I
enter the door of our little house (and it is small, for the five
of us), all my cares and the terrible sights I have seen melt
away. I think sometimes of the ice breaking up on the Albany
River. How it shifted and roared! How the river struggled to
break free! I, in a quieter way, and with much less struggle,
feel free at last. Is it not one of life's beautiful paradoxes that
when we are most bound to the people we love, we are most
free? How my heart lifts when I return home and our
youngest calls out, 'Father! Father's home at last!'"

My one abiding sorrow was to do with Isobel Gunn. She
would not accept the money I sent to the doctor, nor would
she answer my letters. The doctor reported that friends in
Stromness saw her and the little girl, whose name was

Nellie, out digging peats or down at the harbour, selling stockings when a ship came in. They seemed to keep to themselves except for a couple of widows whose men had been at the Bay. They were shabby and obviously poor, but they were clean. They were sometimes seen, of a Sunday, at the very back of the parish church, but they did not mingle and hurried away as soon as the service was over.

Although the parish I served was in the New Town and therefore prosperous, and in truth my wife and I could have spent most of our time taking tea with our respectable parishioners, we spent many hours visiting the "other Edinburgh" in the Grassmarket, the Cowgate and the foul-smelling streets that made up the Old Town. The lodging-houses were the worst, full of transients and criminals, men, women and children all crammed together like herrings in a dank, cold net. "I shall make you fishers of men," said Our Lord, but the fishermen (and women) here were the lodging-house keepers who, with their baits of three pence a night or less, lured into their cellars the wretched of the earth. In Skinner's Close, in Allison Close, in North Gray's Close, they huddled together, shared scraps of shag tobacco and gin, lice and disease.

To say we were not always welcome by those we had come to visit would be an understatement, and we were, as often as not, treated with derision and rough words. But there were enough, particularly of women, who wordlessly reached out a hand to us, clung to us for a moment or two, from some tangle of rags on the floor. And the houses of the poor told the same wretched story. The father and mother sat by what fire there was in a state of apathy or drunkenness, while the oldest child sold fir sticks or lucifers, earning, if lucky, a penny or two a day to help support a family of half a dozen or more.

My wife held filthy babies in her arms or smoothed the brow of the dying and never once turned away in despair or disgust. She made her way back to Inverleith Row, took off her bonnet, put her clothes to one side to be washed, washed herself and began the preparations for supper. Only her high colour, after one of these visits, indicated the extent of her anger and distress.

"The women of this parish," she said more than once, "talk a great deal about the 'deserving poor.' They chastise me for wasting time and energy on those who live in such squalid conditions. Not one will accompany me, not one! And yet they seem confident that their well-scrubbed souls will fly straight up to heaven! Ach, well, at least I can shame them into contributing more to the Poor Funds, and who are they to challenge the minister's wife about how those funds are to be used?"

The hypocrisy of the respectable grated on us both, and I did my best not to judge those of the wretched who turned to drink in order to dull the pain. Poverty breeds apathy; there is a dignity in labour that all but the most hardened criminal must yearn for. We are what we do, and if there is nothing to do then we are nothing. When I thought of Isobel I said to myself, "At least she has found an occupation, and compared with the women I have seen here, her life is not so bad. Perhaps she is right not to accept help. Perhaps it has less to do with what I see as her anger at my 'desertion' of James and more to do with her sense of herself, her dignity. And she knows I am here if she needs me."

Meanwhile my stepdaughters grew older, my shyness at delivering the Sunday sermon lessened and my life, generally speaking, seemed as spacious, comfortable and well-ordered as the broad streets and squares of the New Town. When we could, we took long walks in the surrounding countryside and the Pentland Hills, stopping for simple picnics when the weather permitted. In winter we sat by the fire and read out loud to one another, and sometimes I sat and listened to Margaret and her daughters sing four-part harmony, beautiful madrigals, for they all had been trained in music, except the youngest, but she had a clear voice and a natural talent for song. Strict Calvinists we could never be, for music was part of our nourishment, like bread.

The years slid by—I see them as swans making their stately way along a river, no sudden movements to disturb their progress. There were evenings when, looking at my family, I was moved almost to tears by my good fortune.

I had not forgotten about James. Each year at Christmastime, after my annual note of good wishes to Isobel, I wrote him a letter, c/o Mr. Morton, Former Chief of Albany Fort, c/o The Company of Adventurers, Fenchurch St., London. I told him that I often thought of him, and that I would always look upon him with the fondness of an uncle and hoped one day to see him again. There was never a reply until 1826. "Dear Sir, Please desist in your enquiries. Mr. Morton is dead and, so far as we have been able to ascertain, there was no issue. Yours, etc." It was signed by the general secretary.

And in 1828, a letter from Isobel.

DERE SONE, WEE AR badly of Just Now.

When Nellie was sixteen she left Stromness for Edinburgh. Isobel tried to keep her but it was no use, and perhaps, by then, she was ready for her niece to go. Nellie was young and pretty and clever with her hands; her straw-plaiting was known throughout the district. She also did plain sewing, finishing bedsheets and fine lawn handkerchiefs for the prosperous older ladies in the district whose eyes were not what they once had been.

And Isobel, who herself had fled Orkney in order to have an adventure, perhaps her protests were not so loud and long? Also, she had her pride. There would be no talk of lone-liness or the poverty she could see, like a sinister black figure, appearing in the distance. Her bright hair had faded, but she was still strong and healthy at forty-five. Nellie did ask Isobel to come with her, but she declined, not only because the idea of Edinburgh frightened her (frightened her more than wolves or bears or any natural thing), but also because there was always the chance of a letter—or even the lad himself—arriving at Hamnavoe. In her fancy she saw a brave young gentleman, splendidly dressed, stepping from a jolly boat onto the pier and hastening to make enquiries for a Mrs. Gunn, "my mother." She would not budge.

And so Nellie left alone, with her small bundle—some
samples of her work and two letters of reference, one as
to her character and one as to her skill with needle and
thread—determined to be a dressmaker. Isobel sewed a
sovereign into Nellie's petticoat, a sovereign it had taken her
a year to save, and Nellie went off on a boat headed for Leith.
She also had my address, which Isobel had never used and, as
it so sadly transpired, was not used when it should have been
by Nellie. There was no help coming from Jannet's husband,
for he had joined the navy years before and was lost at sea,
and her grandparents would have nothing to do with her
because she lived with Isobel Gunn.

Nellie was a hard worker and could read and write quite
well (Isobel had insisted she go to the parish school when she
was small), and was confident she would soon find a good
position. We're a nation of wanderers and seafarers, always
have been. And not afraid of hard work either; Nellie was
one of us.

At first she had luck, was soon apprenticed to a dressmaker in Victoria Street, and lodged, with three other girls,
nearby. She also got piece-work from a tailor, men's shirts,
both plain and striped, and she worked on those in the
evenings until her eyes ached. She had to buy her own
thread, but still they brought in a few more shillings. Her
letters to her aunt are full of exuberance: how big the city
is! how grand are the men and women of the New Town!
What fun it is to walk with her friends in the Princes Street
Gardens, the east side, for the west was closed to the
public. She missed the clear air of Orkney, but she loved the

noise and bustle of the place and the innocent flirtations she engaged in on her Sunday promenades. Isobel, who had never carried on a flirtation in her life, was struck by how quickly Nellie had become a sophisticated miss. But she did not worry about her; Nellie was strong-willed but upright. The boys of Stromness had been sniffing around her for years and she had just laughed, saying she had better things in mind than a life of bannocks and babbies. Isobel did not pray for her; she prayed for one thing only.

It is certainly possible that all three of her companions supplemented their incomes with partial prostitution. Edinburgh after the war was not an easy place in which to make a living, and pretty girls like pretty things. Or she may have been approached by someone. She could hardly have been as sophisticated as she appeared in her letters to her aunt. However it came about, the letters stopped in 1827 and Isobel, in desperation, wrote to me in the New Year:

"I think my hart wille brake." Such a cry!

The Old Town, with its towering houses and warrens of apartments, people crammed together, stacks of human beings, often reminded me of the high cliffs of Orkney and the nesting birds, each with its little ledge, however small, to stand on, to eat, sleep, procreate, and also of the doctor's words to my father on that winter evening long ago: "It is the stench that nearly defeats me." I went back to her original lodgings in Victoria Street, but the landlady, very suspicious of my questions, said all four girls had left some time ago and she neither knew nor cared what had happened to them. They were nice enough girls, but she

preferred men—quieter, less inclined to giggles and midnight chatter. No lads throwing pebbles at the windows
after midnight.

"Did they leave separately or together?"

"They quit this place the same time, but after that . . ."
She shrugged. I came away with several unopened letters in
Isobel's hand.

I enquired throughout the Grassmarket and Cowgate,
exhausted every lead. Edinburgh was full of red-headed
girls, both Irish and Scots, full of pretty girls too, in from the
country or from across the water, wanting whatever they
imagined the city had to offer them. Unemployment was
rife, and the newcomers, unless they had a sponsor, soon fell
into poverty worse than they had known at home. But
Nellie, who had marketable skills and at least a rudimentary
education—surely she could survive, even here? Perhaps she
had moved up in the world, not down. I expanded my
enquiries to our side of town, but no one seemed to have
heard of her. The police just smiled politely and asked if I
knew how many girls went missing every year. And now,
with these dreadful murders on their hands, they weren't too
interested in assigning even one man to a private investiga-
tion. However, since I was a man of the cloth, they would see
what they could do.

At this time the city of Edinburgh was also full of
"Resurrectionists," men who robbed new graves in the
middle of the night, opening the coffin, removing the body,
then replacing the earth and grass. The bodies were then sold
to the anatomists, who gave good money for them, eight to

ten pounds for each. The doctors who lectured in anatomy
needed more and more bodies, and although the law stated
that only the corpses of executed criminals could be used
in dissection, they did not enquire too carefully as to the
origins of the corpses sold in Surgeons' Square.

Burke and Hare, two Irishmen who had started out as
navvies working on the Union Canal, hit upon a better way
to make money without doing any digging: they simply
killed their victims and then sold them, sixteen in all, from a
boy of twelve years to his ancient grandmother. When they
were discovered, the entire city was horrified. Robbing
graves was bad enough, but murdering people and pretending they were freshly dead was much, much worse. The
names of Burke and Hare were on everyone's lips in 1829
and thousands turned out to see Burke hanged, thousands to
see him publicly dissected. I had been searching for Nellie
for more than a year.

I knew the names of the girls who had been murdered by
these monsters: everyone knew them, for it was the talk of
the town, Old and New. It never occurred to me that Nellie
might have changed her name.

Then, three weeks later, at the house of a friend of mine,
a doctor and parishioner—he reminded me a great deal of
my father's old friend—I heard about the young beauty who
had brought down Burke and Hare. Something about the
description chilled me to the bone. I asked if it was possible
to see the corpse, and he arranged it.

I saw her only twice, once as a wee babe peeping out
from behind her auntie's skirts and once as a corpse, with all

the pallor and stillness of death upon her, but I knew that
Mary Phipps was Nellie Craig. I wanted to claim her immediately and give her a decent burial, but her dissection had
already begun. And so I made arrangements afterwards to
take the body, by night, in a closed carriage, and give her a
decent burial with a few words spoken over her head. The
police, much to my surprise and eternal gratitude, were very
co-operative, and Nellie's name was never mentioned in
connection with the grisly case. She remains on the books as
Mary Phipps.

The corpse was heavily swaddled—I gave out to the
grave-diggers that she was an accident victim—and smelled
strongly of spirits, for the body had been declared such a
perfect anatomical specimen that Dr. Knox, before the discovery, had kept it preserved in whisky. Later I put up a small
stone, omitting her name, but with the simple phrase, "Yea,
though I walk through the Valley of the Shadow . . ."

If Isobel had only written to me sooner, I could certainly
have helped Nellie. What a dreadful way to die. What had ini-
tiated her slide into prostitution? I had interviewed the
dressmaker to whom she was apprenticed, and she said that
Nellie, at first, had been an excellent worker, but that for the
past six months she had come in late and her sewing often
had to be unpicked and done again. Finally she had to be let
go. I gathered from the tailor that she had continued to work
for him until he, too, dismissed her. Neither the tailor nor
the dressmaker had connected Nellie with the victims of
Burke and Hare; as I said, Edinburgh was full of pretty red-
haired country girls. And of course the name was wrong.

I went neither to the hanging of Burke, dressed in his black "dead man's clothes," nor to his dissection, to which the public was invited, but I was so full of anger I could have killed him myself. Killed them both. Angry too at the anatomists and their greed—more bodies, more bodies, more bodies. I understood how important it was for students of medicine to know what lay beneath the skin, but the constant cry for more bodies led to the Resurrectionists and, finally, to Burke and Hare. Were the doctors not monsters also? I suddenly thought of McTavish, on that winter's day at Albany Fort, wondering if it would have been better for the Natives if the Company of Adventurers had never come to Rupert's Land. Greed persuaded the factors that it was all right to give the Natives rum. Their rivals did it, so they were "forced" to do it as well. Where greed exists and competition for gain, disaster surely follows.

How had they killed her? Did she suffer? I have read her brave letters to Isobel—"a new life," she says in one of them. Soon she would graduate from hems to fancy bodices; nothing could stop her from having her own little shop someday. Now spirited away to a lonely grave, dressed only in swaddling and shroud.

My stepdaughters were also bonny, but they had a loving home and parents to look after them. It is true they ran a chance of being robbed or run down by a carriage, but I doubted they would ever be tempted into prostitution, even the high-class prostitution of the New Town. They were not poor.

After several attempts at letters, I told my wife I must go back to Orkney and deliver this sad news to Isobel in person. My young assistant would see to the Sunday services until my return. My wife pressed my hand and nodded.

"This is not something that can be told in a letter. But be gentle," she warned; "does she need to know everything?"

"Perhaps not."

NELIE IS DED POORE girle and I am on well from hid.

Stromness had changed greatly since last I stepped ashore at Hamnavoe. In 1811 the town was little more than a sprawl of houses along the main street, but now, thanks both to achieving the status of Royal Burgh of Barony in 1817 (which released it from the thrall of Kirkwall, gave it financial independence, a weekly market and an annual fair) and to the introduction of straw-plaiting and some other thriving manufactories, the parish of Stromness had a population of more than twenty-five hundred, and I was told St. Peter's Church, in the town itself, had a congregation of twelve hundred. There were boatyards and inns and far too many public houses. There was even a subscription library, and a cannon, captured from an American privateer, was now fired to announce the arrival of the Honourable Company's ships. All was bustle and noise, but unlike the bustle and noise of that big city where I now made my home, Stromness still had the air of a friendly country town where most, if not all, knew and greeted one another. Isobel did not know I was coming, so I found my own way to where she lived.

On the long journey north I concocted a plausible story that avoided the subject of Nellie's prostitution. I would simply say she had contracted tuberculosis and had eventually succumbed to it. She had not written because she had been too weak. I could even say I had been with her at the end and had held her hand. A minister telling lies? But what possible good could telling the truth accomplish?

And yet, in the end, I did tell her the truth, and we sat and wept together. We dug some heather, to plant upon the grave, wrapping it in a piece of sacking to keep it moist. As we walked across the fragrant, peaty hills there was a part of me that wished never to leave. What had a city to offer compared with the scent of the islands and their clear, uncompromising light?

I was concerned about Isobel, for after the first storm of grief she seemed dangerously subdued. One afternoon, as we walked along the cliffs, she stopped and moved forward, staring down at the wild water pounding the rocks below. I came up quickly and grabbed her arm.

"'Tis a pity it's not myself, instead of Nellie, in the ground."

"You mustn't think that way."

"What do you know of the thorns in my heart?"

"It is not your fault—what happened to Nellie."

"Whose fault is it, then?"

"We make choices," I said, lamely.

She tore her arm away from mine. "Oh, nivver talk to me of choices!"

She began to run and I ran after her.

"Isobel, come back!"

At that, she stopped. I can see her still, standing in her old black skirt out there on the headland, her hair flying about in the wind, seabirds screaming above her.

She clung to me when I reached her.

"Do you think he's a fine young gentleman by now?"

I smiled. "That was Mr. Morton's intention."

"And mine."

"Yes."

"Married, mebbe, with a wee boy of his own?"

"Perhaps."

"Oh!" she cried, "how cruel of Mr. Morton never to send me word!"

I nodded. "A cruel man, yes." I did not wish to tell her, at this terrible time, that Mr. Morton was dead. She had enough to bear.

This time when I took her arm, she did not pull away, and that night, since she seemed less apathetic and somewhat more interested in the world around her, I sat by her side in the rooms she had shared with Nellie, just two rooms on the first floor of a house not far from the harbour, up Brinkie's Brae, and told her a bit about my wife and daughters. I asked if she would come back to Edinburgh with me, said that my wife and I had discussed this and that we wished to offer her a home, permanently or temporarily, as she chose.

She shook her head.

"Would you not like to see where Nellie's buried?"

"A grave is a grave. No, I must stay here."

I was seated in the only chair and she on a wee creepie by my side. The only light was from the cruisie by the bed. She had been knitting as we talked and now she put the half-finished stocking in her lap and took my hand.

"You asked me to wed you once."

"Aye, I did that."

"Out of pity."

"Not out of pity, no."

"What then?"

"Friendship," I said. "The Greeks talked about three kinds of love; they considered friendship the greatest."

"You could never ha' come back here," she said. "No one would ha' given you a living."

"Mr. Morton's letter of dismissal made sure I could never get a living here in any case. He showed it to me: 'little faith and less character.'"

"He said that?"

I nodded.

"That is because you befriended me and the boy." She paused, took up her knitting again. "Sometimes I think 'twas all a dream—Rupert's Land and a' that happened there. But James wasna a dream."

"No. And you did what you thought was best for him."

"James gone, Nellie died: I'm like a cat without her kits. Were it wrong to let him go? You think so, don't you? You think hid was unnatural."

"I think you felt in an impossible position and Mr. Morton knew it."

"I saw us," she said, almost in a whisper, her needles clicking as she talked, as though she were knitting up not a stocking for a sailor but the story of her life. "I saw us cold an' hungry, goin' from door to door with our cruisies on our backs—'Please, madam, a bit o' meal,' 'Please, sir'—and the doors shut in our faces because I was not a decent woman, because I deserved to suffer. I saw us hungry an' cold an' my beautiful boy cryin' from an empty stomach." The tears fell on the wool in her lap.

"There was Jannet."

"I think I musta had a feeling . . . some sense that . . ." She couldn't finish.

"And Margaret and the rest of your family?"

"I wouldna go to them. Nivver."

I went to see the doctor, who was now nearly eighty and no longer the robust man I had known in my childhood. He was still living in Kirkwall, in the old house, but had retired from practice. He possessed an excellent housekeeper, and we feasted on herrings in oatmeal and bere bannock. His daughter looked in once a day. He was disappointed that I had elected not to stay with him, but rather in Stromness, but when I told him about Nellie and my fears for Isobel he understood.

"Can she still support herself by making stockings?"

I smiled. "She says she can, so long as her hands and eyes hold out. I tried to persuade her to come back to Edinburgh with me; Margaret has even sent a note, urging her to come, but no."

"She doesn't expect the long-lost son to show up after all these years!"

"She doesn't expect it, but she longs for it. She even showed me a small cache of money she has put by, to have a fine dress and bonnet should he appear."

"Do you think he will come?"

"No. I think Mr. Morton wanted to cut all ties between James and his mother. I doubt if James Morton even knows that he was once James Scarth, or that he has a mother named Isobel Gunn. He was still very young when I left, and although Mary, his Native foster mother, swore an oath that she would make sure James knew about Isobel, Mr. Morton's intention was clearly to wean the child's affections away from her as well. I can never reconcile myself to the fact that he was such a perceptive artist—he could get the essence of fish, flesh or fowl with a few quick strokes—and yet at heart he was full of self-interest, cared nothing for the feelings of others. It will always be a puzzle to me. It is unconscionable that he has never kept her informed about her son."

"Is it possible that you could enquire?"

"I have enquired, written letters to Mr. Morton c/o the Company, to the secretary of the Company itself, to Albany Fort. All that the Company would tell me was that Mr. Morton had died in 1817, and that so far as they knew there was 'no issue.' How Morton died, or where, they would not disclose. It must have been in London, for he hated the Bay. He would never have stayed on unless his uncle insisted upon it, went back on his promise. I wrote to the SSPCK, for there is an English branch, to see if they could trace Mr. Morton's mother. I am in disfavour with them for having been dismissed, but I thought, being Christians, they might help me. No reply. No reply at all. No doubt Mr. Morton spread some story about my bad influence on the child, and with his uncle as a member of the Committee, he succeeded in making me *persona non grata* both in London and at the Bay."

"Poor lassie."

"If you could have seen her with the boy!" I paused. "I cannot believe that she was preordained to suffer so."

"Do you remember what you asked your father that terrible afternoon at Neverholme Farm?"

"No. What did I say?"

"On the way home, he told me, you turned to him and asked, 'Is that woman one of the damned?'"

"And what was his reply?"

"He held you close for an instant and told you to hush."

"But gave me no answer?"

"But gave you no answer."

The doctor was too frail for the long walk to the cemetery, although he said that at least once a fortnight he went out with horse and cart to "pass an agreeable hour" close by his wife and his old friends. And so I went on my own, knelt down by the graves of my parents and longed for them to be alive and whole again, to advise and comfort me as they had in the past. The wind was still up and it rippled the long grass in the old churchyard as though unseen shapes were gliding rapidly all around me. I lingered until the sun was nearly set, and then in the twilight I walked over the hills and back to Kirkwall, where I had agreed to spend the night. It was longer that way, but my heart was too full to speak, even to greet a fellow traveller along the road.

The next day, carrying the clump of white heather for Nellie's grave, I left for Edinburgh. Isobel came down to see me off, and I could not help noticing how, after all this time, children still pointed at her and women turned their heads. I wondered how often she went out of doors.

"Thank you for comin'," she said and shook my hand quite formally. Then from her pocket she took a parcel.

"What is this?"

"Open it later. 'Tis for yersel' and yer good wife."

It was a pair of worsted stockings for each of us.

I did not see her again for thirty-three years.

BEING A MAN, I COULD NOT imagine the struggle that went on in Isobel's breast. It was only years later, after I related to my dear wife the whole sad story while sitting by the fire on a chill Edinburgh evening, that the full weight of Isobel's decision was brought home to me.

After she had listened quietly for an hour, she told me, head down and concentrating fiercely on the piece of work she had picked up at the beginning of my narrative, that there had been another daughter, between the second and the third, a child who lived long enough only to open her eyes and close them again.

"I still think of that child," she said softly, "imagine what she might have been like. Not constantly, but occasionally, most especially when the anniversary of her birth comes round. The pain of that loss is always with me. How much greater must the pain have been to Isobel Gunn, with a happy, healthy child who already called her Mother. How hard to give him up for what she saw as his greater good. How she must miss him still. How she must hope that some-day he will come to Orkney, if only to acknowledge her sacrifice and thank her."

"I wish with all my heart that it were so."

"You think it will never happen?"

"Mr. Morton was a strange man, and he had ways of keeping the Company's servants quiet. Whatever the hard-ships, it was a good job, signing on with the Company, with far better wages than an ordinary labourer could get at home—or even a skilled labourer such as an armourer or a carpenter. And there was nothing, really, to spend your wages on. To be threatened with dismissal . . . well, it would take a strong man to stand up to that."

"You stood up to him."

"Oh, aye, and I was a fool to do so."

"How so?"

"I never thought he'd dismiss me so soon; I somehow assumed I was necessary to his plan. I thought I would have time to work something out."

THE YEARS WENT BY. Her eyes began to fail, and then her hands became arthritic. She could no longer work a sock. And now the vision

she had had so long ago, the nightmare of begging from door to door, came true: a skrankie old woman in shuizly clothes, always cold-bitten. She was put on the parish roll as one of the Destitute Poor, barefoot most of the time, a caisie on her back. A Company widow took pity on her and gave her a small chamber in her house in return for washing clothes (ach! how it tortured her hands!) and tending the kail yard. Still, she had to beg for bere-meal for her porridge.

All in Stromness knew her, and she took to proclaiming herself to those who opened their door: "Have pity on puir Isobel Gunn, once loyal servant to the Company of Adventurers. Have pity!"

"Shameless," the housewife might say to herself, but many a door that was shut to others was opened to her cry and a measure of meal handed out. She never said a thank-you, just nodded and limped away.

Sometimes, when her belly rumbled with hunger and all she could boil up was weak tea, she remembered the taste of fat geese, of deer meat, of salt fish. Remembered Mary and her tipi; children playing like puppies; women cutting rabbit-skin into lengths for sewing; beading moccasins and leggings; smoking the long clay pipes. She had been happy with those women, even though she could speak little of their language. Where was Mary now, her true sister, her faithful friend?

Remembered James. Always remembered James, even the smell of him and the pull of his mouth on her breast. Still went down to the harbour at Hamnavoe when the ship came in, not to ask, any more, "Whit news, whit news?" but just to be there, to see the tall three-masted ship, to be one of the crowd. Stood there like an old crow, a hoodie, in her rusty clothes. When she thought of James, she was ashamed of her old clothes and wild hair. Who would want to say "Mither" to such a one as she?

Yet in her heart she knew he had not forgotten her and would come home when the time was right, a grown man now, no doubt with a wife and grown sons. She must keep going on her weefly legs, left foot, right foot, left foot, right foot, over the cold cobbles of the street, never minding the children who followed her calling, "Isobel Gunn! Isobel Gunn!"

I DID NOT SEE HER AGAIN until 1862, when a letter arrived in an unfamiliar hand. It was from a doctor at the Balfour Hospital in Kirkwall; Isobel had asked him to contact me. He enclosed a barely decipherable note. I reached her a few days before she died, and now I have sat up through the eight days of the lyke-wake as I promised. I'm an old man and I'm weary.

O, MY DERE, MY DERE, my dere Blissings on you all ways til we meat a gaine.

SHE INSISTED UPON RETURNING to her room in Helihole. James might yet come, might enquire where he could find his mother, Mrs. Isobel Gunn.

"Promise me," she whispered, in her dry voice. "Promise!"

I thought the journey might kill her, and the young doctor shook his head, but we Orkney folk have always bowed to the wishes of the dying. I made the necessary arrangements—a cart padded with blankets and a gentle horse to pull it. I admonished the driver to go slowly, promised to pay him by the hour, however long it took.

She lay swaddled in warmth, eyes closed and scarcely breathing, as we set off very early in the morning through the town. Past the cathedral built to honour my namesake, the murdered earl, past the remains of the Bishop's Palace and the palace built by the tyrant Patrick Stewart. Then we were soon out into the countryside and on the road to Orphir. As we passed by the old manse, I thought of a small boy and his father who were set one afternoon for a country ramble but were directed instead to a place of such despair it changed the boy's life forever and entangled him in the life of the dying woman who lay beside him.

I glanced up at Ward Hill and saw—or fancied I saw, my sight is poorly now—another small boy at the very top, staring out across the bay towards Scapa Flow. I did not ask the driver to turn onto the path leading to the cemetery; I had made my farewells to my parents the day before. Each mile we passed, each field and farmhouse and stone wall, I thought to myself, I shall never come this way again. My bones were to lie in Edinburgh, beside the dear woman who had brought me so much happiness and comfort. I could not believe in the Resurrection, except as a figure of speech—that all have the potential to be transformed by love—and yet I wished my body to lie next to the remains of my wife. It saddens me to think that Isobel must lie alone.

The day gradually darkened as we made our slow progress towards Stromness, but the rain and the wind held off until we reached the street called Helihole and Isobel's room near the top. We set her down carefully; I thanked the driver and paid him off. He was a youngish man, a farmer, and he asked me as he left, "Be har your sister?"

"Aye," I answered, "my sister."

I lit some candles and only then did she open her eyes. "One in th' window," she whispered. "Please." Then, as I did what she had asked, "Thank you."

As she slept, I thought who, looking down at this frail figure, this sack of skin and bone, would ever believe this was once a young lad called John Fubbister, who learned to chop wood and shoot a Company gun with the best of the men at the Bay? Our ancient bodies are like the mouldy and tattered bindings on old books full of wondrous tales. She who lay there could be any old Orkney woman who had never lived more than a few hundred yards from where she was born. I had asked her once why she called herself John Fubbister; she said it was the name of a boy who had fallen off the cliff and drowned when she was a child. It just popped into her head.

Ach, so much of this tale has links to water. Not surprising, I suppose, when we are surrounded by it. Is there a child on any of these islands who has not paddled in the tide pools or collected shells to use as animals or armies in his infant games? Is there an Orkney child who has never gorged

himself on sillocks, smoked or fresh? Who has never been in
a boat? Is there a grown man or woman, in exile somewhere,
who has never longed to smell the tangle one more time?
The Bible says ashes to ashes, and rightly so, for we are more
or less bound to the earth, puir gill-less, fin-less creeturs that
we are, and even the hardiest fishermen, those who venture
into the icy waters of Greenland or the Davis Strait, even the
mightiest captain of a ship, know that these wooden boats
and the men within them are only tolerated by the sea. Once
overboard we quickly drown.

And yet we love it, cannot live far from its seductive
dangers.

Tomorrow Isobel will be buried in the old cemetery on
the headland, the sounds of the sea below her and the misty
scarves of the haar rising up and over her grave. Her own
folk are buried near Neverholme Farm—except for her
mother, of course—but Isobel has had no intercourse with
any of them for more than fifty years and I choose to bury
her here, in the parish where she lived. I am sad and sorry
she never saw her son again after she stepped into the sloop
at Albany all those years ago. Someone knows where he
is—or was—but the Company keeps its secrets. Where did
he go after Mr. Morton so suddenly died? I hope for his
sake—and even more for the sake of his mother and her
sacrifice—that life has been good to him, wherever he may
be; that he was loved, *is* loved; and that somewhere in the
back of his mind, whatever lies he has been told, there is
some sweet recollection of those who loved him in his
infancy.

Before she died, Isobel awoke from a doze and gripped my hand, which was covering hers as she slept.

"Magnus?"

"I'm here."

"Tell me true. Will I see my boy, one day, in heaven?" Her eyes, bright with fever, seemed to scour the inside of my soul. How could I lie to her?

"Ach, of course you will."

"And Nellie?"

"And Nellie as well."

"And will God forgive me for all my sins?"

"How could He not?"

She fell back, exhausted but with a small smile. That was the last we spoke together, although she kept her hand in mine. Within the hour she was dead.

It is long past midnight now and my vigil soon is over. I have foregone the kisting, and so she lies, until tomorrow, in her own narrow bed. The wind howls around and under the door, making the candles dance and flicker, casting bizarre shadows on the walls. I can hear a little mouse, possibly two, nibbling at something in the corner, perhaps crumbs from the supper I had sent in. He doesn't bother me—he is a small affirmation that life goes on, and why shouldn't the body of my tale have a reference to rodents near the end as it did at the beginning? I wonder whatever happened to the *Castorologia*.

When people in Edinburgh who have heard I was at the Bay ask, "What was it like?" I'm hard put to make a reply—or a reply that would satisfy them. What I want to say is simply this: "I taught school. I learned to fire a gun and walk in snowshoes. I twice saw a sun dog. I met a woman who wanted to live as a man, until she had a child. I was dismissed. I returned to Scotland. My life began."

This would not do. What they want are stories of the great fur trade, of Canadians and savages and country wives. What I give them, usually, is mostly silence. I smile and say, "Ach, it was all so long ago."

Tonight, when I think of the men at the Bay, I see, first, their hands: hands chopping, rowing, shooting, hammering, grinding, baiting, sewing, sweeping, packing and repacking. And the hands of the women also busy at their tasks.

My hands pointing to the letters of the alphabet.

Isobel's hands, lifting James from the schoolroom floor, caressing him.

Mr. Morton's hands holding his charcoal pencil.

The flames from the candles flicker in the draughts, cast shadows like busy fingers on the wall.

I am an old man, and my old man's thoughts circle back upon themselves like a dog preparing to lie down.

I am deeply sorry I could do so little for Isobel Gunn. Although I never felt she was anything but misguided to give up her child to Mr. Morton, she knew a great deal more about poverty than I, knew it from the inside, and I cannot, in the end, condemn her for this brave and foolish act. Scarth I detest; he deserved his drowning, although I pray I am wrong about Isobel's hand in that. But even Scarth I cannot completely write off, for out of his bestial act came James, who brightened all our lives at Albany and who once buried his face in my neck and called me Father.

He knew nothing of the letters, sitting in a folder tied up with grey ribbon, in the Company's offices in London. His father had told him, "Your mother died in childbirth." He did not believe this, and yet never asked, "Where, then, lies her grave?" The move from Albany Fort to Fort Garry, his father's death, his removal to the care of a stern, uncompromising couple he could never learn to love—each upheaval left him more silent, more alone.

Yet every so often there were strange dreams, as vivid as memories, and once, at the Forks, a shabby woman scarred by smallpox. His hand, of its own volition, reached out to touch her face; his fingers remembered—something. Reached out, but she, a stranger, shocked by the gesture, increased her pace and hurried away from him.

EPILOGUE

IN 1938 A BOY FROM *Winnipeg looked out his bedroom
window at the snow piled high against the house and dreamt
not of hockey games, but of running away to sea. He was the
youngest of four brothers, and not only the youngest, but also of a
different physical type, with his mother's small frame and dark
hair. His father and his older brothers were big, stocky males, and
the brothers liked to tease him and call him the Pipsqueak.*

*There was not much money to spare in this family, and except
for underwear at Christmas and a new pair of shoes at the beginning of school (he loved the smell of his new shoes, loved going
downtown to the shoestore with his mother, standing up with his
feet in the X-ray machine, where, looking down, he could see his
foot bones floating in a milky green sea) he never owned anything
that hadn't been "passed down." "Don't worry," said his mother
as she altered pantcuffs and shirtsleeves, biting the thread neatly
with her teeth, "you'll no doubt have a big growth spurt later on,
and even if you don't, no matter; God gave you enough brains*

to get on with, and you're as quick on your feet as any lad I know."

"Am I adopted?" he asked when he was ten years old.

"No, no. You look too much like my grandfather, rest his soul. And you look like me as well. My grandfather said his father was adopted, but that he never talked about it much, except he thought his real father was not his real father. He thought maybe he had been kidnapped by the Indians and rescued by the man who said he was his father. He remembered an Indian woman who was kind to him, but who was sent away. My grandfather had a pair of child's moccasins with beautiful beadwork that he kept in the dresser drawer, wrapped up in paper, so perhaps that part is true."

"Where are those moccasins now?"

"I have no idea. Maybe they got thrown away or lost. My family was never much for keeping things. I can remember my grannie reading a letter from one of her sisters, then tossing it in the stove. I come from some other strain; I'm a saver."

She smiled. "And when I said my prayers at night, my grandfather called them my bonie-words. 'Up you go now and don't forget your bonie-words.' My grannie didn't say that. Strange."

"And you never asked him?"

"Never."

"I would have asked him!"

"I'm sure you would. You were born with a question mark planted in your brain."

"What happened to that man? The one who said he was his father?"

"He died, I guess. My father never was very interested in all that ancient history, so that's the sum total of all I know about it."

"Do you think the boy's father was a sailor?"

"Oh, I don't think so. A settler probably."

"Then he would have come by ship; he would have crossed the ocean."

"Oh, yes. Any white people here would have crossed the ocean."

"Someday," the boy said (he knew he could confide in her), "I'm going to be a sailor."

"Are you, darling?" she said, and smiled at him. "Are you going to sail away from me?"

"Don't worry," he said, patting her arm, "it won't be for a long time yet."

He wasn't sure where the idea of being a sailor had come from; he seemed to have been born with it, he whose notion of the sea was got from books. He did not know that many boys had such dreams, but few acted upon them, especially boys from Winnipeg, so his parents were astonished to discover a note one morning saying he had left to "see the world."

"He'll be home tomorrow," said his father, a nice, unimaginative man.

"Imagine the Pipsqueak, roaming the world on his own," said his eldest brother. "Shall we have a wager on how far he'll get before he turns around?"

They finished breakfast and went off to their various employments, laughing and shaking their heads. But the mother sat silent and afraid; she knew he would not return until he had accomplished what he set out to do.

At the end of the week they went to the police, but the boy was small enough, ordinary enough, quick enough, to escape notice. His older brothers, who had never been out of Winnipeg (although they, too, would soon be gone), would have been surprised to see how clever

*he was at getting on and off trains without being seen, how polite he
was when he turned up at back doors offering to work for his supper.*

*He made it to Montreal and from Montreal, God knows how, to
England. On a ship, of course, but what ship, and how would he have
found the money? As a stowaway perhaps? Once in England he spent
nearly a year working with fishermen out of Hastings, learning
about winds and tides, taking his first sips of ale, learning to swear
and mend nets. He smoked Player's cigarettes and let his hair grow
long. When he felt he was ready, he talked his way (orphan, birth
certificate lost, just try me, sir) onto a battleship as one of 120 "Boys"
who apprenticed to the Royal Navy. The ship was due to have a
shakedown cruise for two years in the Mediterranean, but when war
broke out it was decided that she would be reassigned, with the rest
of the Home Fleet, to the safe northern waters of Scapa Flow.*

*Our boy, now an official Boy and calling himself Frank Player
(Frank for his father, Player for the cigarettes he smoked) loved his
new life and had finally written to his mother to say so and to add
how sorry he was if he had caused his family pain. He could not tell
them where he was except to say he was apprenticed to the Royal
Navy and hoped to make his career at sea. When this bloody (crossed
out "bloody") war was over, he assured her, he would come for a visit
and tell her all about his adventures.*

*He closed with love and handed in the letter, flap not stuck
down, as instructed, and felt a burden lift from his heart. Soon his
family would know he was alive and well.*

*The oldest of the Boys was seventeen, the youngest fourteen,
and, concerned about their education in more than sea-knowledge
and ship-knowledge, the captain appointed a leading seaman as an
assistant schoolmaster. They were to keep logs and he would correct*

their spelling and other mistakes. The Boys did as they were told—more or less—but in their spare time they had contests to see who could stay longest in the frigid water of the Flow, who knew the most swear words, who could tell the biggest lies about his experience with girls. Like the rest of the ship's complement, they were a bit fed-up at being stuck up in Orkney, this God-forsaken place, when they ought to be out there on the open seas, doing battle with the enemy.

At 10:30 on the night of Friday the thirteenth of October, 1939, the ship's broadcasting system played "Goodnight, My Love" and all but the men on watch began to settle down. The riding lights had been painted blue and the portholes had been covered. The ship, from the shore, was virtually invisible.

At 1:04 a.m. on the fourteenth, the first torpedo struck; at 1:16, the second. Soon there was fire and frantic calling-out as the power failed and the ship began to roll over like some gigantic sperm whale mortally harpooned. More than eight hundred men died that night, three-quarters of all those on the ship, and of the 120 Boys, only thirty survived. (But they were not the only ones heard calling for their mothers in the darkness.)

Men on fire fell like lucifers into the frigid water. There was fire all around, and those who did survive, kicking their way up out of portholes, leaping away as the ship rolled, had to contend not just with the cold but also with the oily film that coated them black and made it difficult to breathe.

Our boy did not survive, but died amidships, going the wrong way in the darkness. His bones lie forever at the bottom of Scapa Flow, along with most of the other dead. A few items were found along the shore in the following weeks—seaboots, hats, a bugle—

before the navy dropped a net over the wreck so that the bodies of the dead would not come floating to the surface.

Our boy's mother had received his letter, his only letter, and kept it until she died. His brothers came back from the war—one minus a hand but still, there they were, soon with wives and kiddies around the dining-room table at Christmas, at Easter. She knew she was lucky; there were women who had lost husbands, lost all their sons. She should be grateful—was grateful.Why then did she cry so easily? Why then did she feel, so often, as though she had swallowed a stone?